THE NEW BIZARRO AUTHOR SERIES

PRESENTS

KING SPACE
VOID

Anthony Trevino

Eraserhead Press
Portland, OR

ERASERHEAD PRESS
P.O. BOX 10065
PORTLAND, OR 97296

WWW.ERASERHEADPRESS.COM

ISBN: 1-62105-203-6

Anthony Trevino is an artist I haven't worked with or known for as long as some of the others in this year's New Bizarro Author series. I met him briefly at the previous year's Bizarrocon, then he asked me to edit a book of his. It was a good read and a pleasure to work on. Not as weird as Eraserhead is used to but a damn fine book. I could see in Anthony a lot of good qualities as well as just being a talented writer, which he definitely is. His prose is good and he knows how to tell a story.

Anthony took my novella writing workshop. During that workshop, we went through various book pitches and one of them really intrigued me. The idea of people powering a planeteating entity was extremely cool, obviously indebted to the great Jack Kirby but from a fresh perspective. We worked hard to find what angle this book was going to take on that and from there, Anthony discovered a whole other narrative underneath his existing one and that narrative has sprung to life in these pages. If you like weird science fiction, you're going to enjoy this book. It's one of two books this year that are close to genre fiction but possessing a dreaminess that takes them from that place and into the realm of Bizarro.

This book is cool. I say that about all these books. It's always true.

— Garrett Cook, Editor

Acknowledgements

First and foremost, I want to thank Garrett Cook for taking a chance on me. This journey wouldn't have been possible without his encouragement, editorial expertise, and advice— I'm forever in your debt, my friend. I'd also like to thank Mark and Shannon Fogg for never letting me give up on the dream; Brandon Freese and Kai Martin who listened to me ramble on into the late hours, while I fleshed out some clunky plot points; Everyone at Eraserhead for making this an amazing experience; The entire Suicide Squad (NONE OF US FUCKING DIED!); all the writers I've learned from over the last few years: Cody Goodfellow, J. David Osborne, David Agranoff, Adam Cesare, John Skipp, and many more—you might not have realized it, but y'all have influenced the hell out of me; and lastly, a big galactic bear hug goes out to the Buddy System. We still don't know what your deal is, but it's cool.

For my brother and best friend, Andy Strickland.

I wouldn't be alive if it weren't for you, dude.

Chapter One

A severed arm crashed into the top of Dane's skull.

The entire shaft shook. He braced himself on the railing of the circular walkway. More debris from the devoured planet fell through the chamber of King Space Void's massive stomach and into the energy converter.

When it was over Dane turned to see the culprit behind the pain forming in his head. The arm was long, muscular. Circular designs that pulsed red swirled from the stump down to its wrist. He didn't realize it at first, but Dane was holding his own arm, gripping it tight, wondering what it must have been like to feel helpless as the mouth of a giant god blotted out the sun of his or her planet.

Spooked, Dane scooped up the arm, tossed it down the shaft, and took the elevator back up to his room, ignoring the image of the hand falling away.

It almost looked as if it were waving goodbye.

***

"By his grace I am alive, and by his grace we will survive."

Dane recited the words along with the priest and the rest of King Space Void's citizens. Every week four lambs were brought out from their covenant. The covenant raised and taught them that their sacrifices were the most valuable; to give up one's self entirely to further a cause was a selfless act and in doing so, they would reach the Edge much sooner than those left aboard, puling levers and cleaning the massive body of their lord.

Two of the priest's mentees, young women in blue robes, pulled the top of the priest's skull off, set it into a steel container. While one of the mentees held the skull-bowl, the other attached two cables to the priest's brain.

The priest crossed his arms, hummed to himself. Then, he threw his arms wide. "Good people of King Space Void. I am here to show you the face of bravery and loyalty. In these men and women to my right, you see not just your fellow citizens, but true believers in our mission to the Edge. Let us not be ungrateful for the Master's hand in taking us from a dying world and straight toward Shangri-La."

The priest raised his hands upward. "Say it with me, good people. Our journey will not be in vain. For the Master is kind and will free us from pain. We endure in this life, so that in the next, we can live in peace."

Dane didn't know how the Priest was able to speak to the master through the conductors sticking into his head, but he spoke with such fervor and conviction, that Dane believed anything was possible.

"Are you there, Master?"

"Yes," came the voice from the speakers mounted along the inside of the gut.

"These three before you have come to relinquish themselves from their corporeal prisons, in your honor. Together, they wish to feed the machine."

The citizens of King Space Void chanted the last three words over and over, Dane included.

"Lord, do you accept this offering?"

"Simon. Katrina. Danielle. You are doing a brave thing to further our cause. For this we thank you. May you go in peace and we will see you on the other side."

The lambs stepped up to the edge of the walkway. One by one they left the metal floor. Never once did they scream. Not even when they landed in the maw of the hungry 'grynder awaiting them at the bottom.

***

Up in his room, Dane stepped into the shower stall. A red light went on above his head. Anxiety turned his guts into a bow. No matter how many times he went through the full body search, the inspector snakes made him nervous. They were necessary, though. The Master wanted to ensure that the worker's in the gut weren't hoarding valuables that might have gotten lost in the ductwork—or worse, plotting against King Space Void.

Three port holes opened up: one underneath his genitals; one behind him; and another directly in front of him. Dane knew the drill; legs spread and mouth wide.

"Please stand still," said an automated voice from the speakers outside the stall.

The first inspector snake, greased in anesthetic, slid down his throat, numbing his esophagus. Cold tubing invaded his rectum. Reflexively, Dane bit down. Heat spread through his lower abdomen, while the third snake prowled the length of his body to see if anything was hidden behind the thin walls of his skin.

Dane wondered if anyone was ever stupid enough to steal from the Master—he hadn't heard of their being any attempts. No one would jeopardize the system; much like a parasite needs a host, the citizens of King Space Void needed their master despite working conditions that often split the skin of their hands and polluted their lungs.

In the thirty years that Dane had been on King Space Void, few had tried to leave—the last group that sought to forge their own way found out first-hand how unforgiving life outside the walls of their floating deity could be.

Dane remembered watching the small shuttle leave the hangar bay high above them. The mutineers had taken a small scout ship; intended for nothing other than bringing back valuable specimens before King Space Void swallowed the planet whole. However, none aboard were pilots and within minutes the shuttle lost power and plummeted into the black like a snowflake down a well.

It was, however, interesting that the Master chose to not act out against them. Instead he let them leave; which had more of an impact on the rest of King Space Void's workers than had the entire group been executed. It was the Master's way of showing them that beyond these walls there was only death and non-existence.

It was enough to keep Dane from thinking about what life might be like outside the walls of King Space Void— although he wondered what it was like up at the to; to be in the presence of the Master would be the highest honor.

When the inspector snakes finished their probe they retreated back to their wall-slots. Dane stood for a moment listening to King Space Void hum. Fire burned in his lungs and he felt a strong urge to void himself in the stall. Instead he braced himself against the wall-tiles, breathed slow and deep until his body's natural reaction to invasion subsided.

Dane tried to open the shower door, found it locked.

Annoyed, he shook the handle harder. The glass vibrated in its frame.

"What's with this shit?"

The speakers above crackled, drooled a string of white noise, and then the familiar voice of the Master filled the bathroom.

"Dane Shipps; Worker 1255."

"Yes, my lord?"

"We must discuss the contents that were found in your body inspection."

"I took nothing, Master. I assure you."

Dane felt a tremor ripple through his body. He thought about the last ten minutes of his shift. He did everything that was expected of him—even after being hit with a severed limb. There was no way he screwed something up or slipped so much as a screw into his grey jumpsuit.

"This is not about stolen property, Dane Shipps. We know that you have done your job appropriately and disposed of the waste. This is about what you felt, so to speak."

"I don't understand."

"The arm. When you looked at it. What did you feel?"

"Nothing."

Silence. The temperature in the room began to climb. Sweat speckled Dane's body. Mentally, he chastised himself for the way he felt. It was just a fucking arm. He'd seen bloodshed before, albeit rarely, but that didn't matter. What mattered to him was doing a good job, doing what he could to bring his people to the Edge.

"Do not lie, Worker 1255. What you felt was fear. Do you remember the lessons about what fear does to us?

Dane hung his head, chin to chest. He didn't know where to avert his eyes, so he closed them. He wanted to shrink himself into a ball, swirl down the drain, and be lost forever.

"I admit to feeling a certain emotion, Master. For that, I am sorry."

"This is a warning, Worker 1255. Those aboard King Space Void need to be tough; resilient in their work if we are to survive our journey to the edge. Just because your job is to turn screws and clean garbage from the interior does not mean you will not be called upon to perform other tasks. It doesn't matter what they are, you must do them, without hesitation and without question. Do you understand?"

Dane shook his head up and down like a puppet with a broken neck. "Yes, I understand."

"Good. You are a valuable worker, 1255. What you do matters. Without you, we would be one step closer to death. Now, join the rest of your crewmates in the Room of Aphrodite. This slip-up will be waived."

"Thank you, Master," Dane said.

The voice cut out. Dane's bowels liquefied and his body burned. He didn't know whether to shit himself or throw up. He slowly bent down to sit on the wet floor of the shower stall. He had never been given a formal warning before. The fact that it happened left him shaken and confused.

He hoped this moment would not lead to him being dropped down into the 'grynder himself. What did the Master do to those that stepped out line? There were rumors, sure; that they were fed into the 'grynder from a different port beneath them; or worse, their skin was removed and integrated into King Space Void's. Dane had seen neither; had only been the recipient of hearsay, but the stories were enough to make his head swim with the possible punishments that awaited him if he screwed up again.

Another, more likely thought, wormed its way into Dane's head. Would the rest of his crew know that he'd been reprimanded? Shamed in the confines of his shower? What would they think of him if they did? Dane didn't want to be the cause of any rumors or the subject of ridicule. Unity was how they all survived. To act outside of what was expected would only lead to chaos and extinction.

That was not Dane. He was a team player and a citizen of King Space Void; a valuable one.

He was Dane Shipps, worker 1255.

And he had a job to do; an image to uphold.

Slowly, Dane pushed himself up, dressed, and headed to the third floor to meet the rest of his crew, a new revitalized desire to impress the Master imprinted at the forefront of his mind.

Chapter Two

Dane held the vanilla shisha smoke in until it felt like his lungs would pop. A hazy screen of smoke obscured the faces around him. Happy that he didn't fall into a coughing fit, he eased back on the soft circular, grey couch. Thick smoke made an ethereal trail from between his lips. Athena and Clark, two of his favorite crew members, snuggled next to him, stroked his shoulders and knees. The anxiety of his earlier encounter with the master subsided.

Grier snatched the hose from Dane's hand. "Another cycle finished, friends." The deformed worker sucked in a lungful of the sweet tobacco, exhaled. "By his grace I am alive, and by his grace we will survive."

Dane and the rest of them repeated the mantra.

"As long as we do what, brothers and sisters?"

"Feed the machine," they all yelled in unison.

"Damn right."

Grier was the only other crew member on King Space Void that could rival Dane's work ethic. The puffy scar tissue that ran across his arms and face proved that. Even though there were times when Dane had to pick up the slack because Grier was sleeping in the ductwork, a pheromone mask pulled tight over his face, pants around his ankles.

Dane never brought these incidents up. The Master held them to the laws of King Space Void, but down in the gut there were other, less official rules. Shining a light on another worker's failing would only create a feud. So, whether you were on or off-shift it was in your best interest to be well-

16

liked. Stanislaw Ellis—Slaws to the crew—found this out when Grier, realized Slaws was spending a lot time alone in the Aphrodite with a woman Grier had taken a liking to.

To everyone else this wasn't an issue. Monogamy was frowned upon by the Master, unless of course you were able to prove that your partnership was beneficial to the mission—therefore couples were sparse aboard King Space Void. Despite this belief, Grier became angrier and angrier as the weeks passed. One day, as debris from another swallowed civilization tumbled down the shafts, Slaws had *accidentally* stood too close to the railing and ended up mulch for the 'grynder.

The Room of Aphrodite took up an entire floor in King Space Void's gut. It was meant as an escape, a place where you could unwind off-the-clock and forget about anything bothering you. They were provided all kinds of luxuries. From treats laced with aphrodisiacs to the spirit boxes, which gave trapped souls the chance to possess one's body. The latter was the ultimate experience of relinquishing control and succumbing to the will of something beyond yourself; although Dane had never seen anyone try it. The amount of time spent was up to the individual; if you didn't have work, then you could stay for hours or even days—the Master was generous in that way.

"I heard that we're passing through an asteroid belt in a few hours," Grier said. "Glad I'm not on shift for that."

Caspere, skeletal-skinny, but fast and efficient, nodded in agreement. "I hope they shut the Master's eyes."

Dane's head felt light, almost empty. Tension bled from overworked muscles. He felt himself drift off like he was floating in a void. Clark and Athena massage his tired limbs. He knew he had only the Master to thank for this life. It was a reward for ensuring King Space Void kept moving, kept sustaining life for those aboard, and their lord above.

Dane hoped that one day he could meet the Master face-to-face, express his gratitude. The Master's tangible body had long been destroyed, but his energy and consciousness resided in the head of King Space Void, preserved for eternity. Dane would never live for as long as the Master, but he had hoped to make a significant impact in the history of King Space Void—even a footnote in their story would make him proud.

The circular platform that held the hookah hummed. Holes opened up all around the base to produce saucers that held wedges of multicolored gelatin. The lights of the Aphrodite dimmed until all Dane could see were cloudy shapes all around him. Everyone shifted in the room to make new friends, except Dane.

Too comfortable to move, he moaned, as his teeth cut through the dessert. Kiwi and lime spread across his tongue. A wave of pleasure jettisoned up his spine and burst at the base of his skull like fireworks.

It was encouraged, but not required, for members of King Space Void to spend time enjoying each other in the Room of Aphrodite. It was another perk for their hard labor. And he loved the feeling of tongues gliding across soft flesh; fingers prodding hidden spaces; teeth nipping lips and leaving small lines of blood behind like passionate reminders.

So why was he feeling off tonight, Dane wondered. The arm flashed in his mind again. The way it tumbled, lifeless and inanimate, down into the maw of the Whatchugrynder.

Hands that were not Dane's gripped his thighs and the image of the arm disappeared. He grew hard. The hands slid upward to knead his groin. A wet tongue grazed his neck, while Dane's hand found a bare muscular chest beside him. His fingers dropped downward until they found a waist-band and pulled the man toward him.

Moans filtered throughout the room along with the sound of zippers being opened and clothes being shucked. Dane continued to pull his faceless lover toward him, happy when their lips connected. The hands that had been at his crotch now glided up underneath his shirt. They felt tender as they pressed down on his stomach. The tongue of his second partner explored his mouth, drifted across his teeth. Suddenly, the second set of hands disappeared into his pants and began to work him over like a determined sculptor.

Another crew member sat next to him. Dane looked over to see that in their lap was a spirit box. The crew member's thumbs rubbed the rough edges and tops of the box that looked as if it were made from tar.

"What do you think, Dane?"

The crew member's face was a charcoal sketch, but Dane recognized the voice. It was Fattahipour from the morning crew. Odd, Dane thought to himself. Fattahipour usually kept away from the Aphrodite, choosing to stay inside and learn more about the history of King Space Void rather than interacting with his fellow citizens.

Fattahipour went on talking before Dane had a chance to respond.

"Something happened to me the other night, Dane." Fattahipour kept massaging the spirit box. "I had a dream. A dream about us; where we're going."

"You saw the edge?"

"No. No, nothing like that."

"What'd you see?"

"Oblivion, Dane. I saw oblivion. We're heading for something awful," Fattahipour said. "That's why I figured, why not see what these boxes are all about. We already live on layers of death, but maybe the other side holds more promise."

The severed arm tried to creep back into Dane's head, pollute his good time. He pushed it out, focused on Fattahipour who was pulling the box slowly open. A small light emanated from it, further intoxicated everyone close by. Lit up by the box's glow, Fattahipour's silver hair turned almost bone white. His eyes, and those around them, were honed in on the spirit manifesting before them. Dane felt the pull on his mind; he didn't just want to see inside of it, he *needed* to.

Dane fell into the moment.

A blue face began to take shape in the box. It seemed friendly, grateful for being let out.

Work. Play. Work. Play. He really didn't have anything to fear or worry about.

Twin orbs of gold light formed in eye sockets of the face. The higher Fattahipour lifted the lid the more the face stretched and moaned. Dane couldn't take his eyes off it. Even though it didn't speak, he felt all the pleasures the spirit offered, all of the ecstasy available to him if he would just relax and submit.

This was life aboard King Space Void, and everything was great.

Until the alarms went off.

Chapter Three

"Workers 1250 to 1257, please report to the bridge."

Walking out of the Aphrodite in his current state was a bit like sleepwalking out of a wet dream. Dane's erection throbbed and he couldn't shake the euphoria surging through him from the aphrodisiacs and what had been hiding in the spirit box before Fattahipour closed. Still, Dane was eager to please the Master.

He stepped over the rest of the Aphrodite's patrons, watching them enjoy their day off. A set of red nails dug furrows across broad shoulders. Moans rang out from different areas as bodies were played like instruments, working to the same climactic crescendo.

Emergency crew workers were supposed to be pulled at random, but Dane knew that was bullshit. The Master called on his best to solve any issues that might get out of hand. He looked at the faces dutifully striding toward the elevator with him. Every single one of them had proved themselves throughout their time aboard. None of them possessed any kind of special abilities that outshined the average person. They were simply men and women who would not be broken down by work, but instead threw everything they had into making sure their world never stopped moving.

Dane's chest swelled with pride. He smiled to himself. Despite the issue from earlier, he was still one of the Master's favorites.

"By his will I am alive," Dane whispered, "And by his will, I survive."

***

They packed themselves into the elevator and rode it to the top. The living units built directly into the gut-walls winked by. Dane tried to glimpse the faces of the workers performing maintenance, but the elevator moved too fast.

"Anyone know what this is about?"

"Guys up at the top probably forgot to close up shop before we hit the belt," Grier said.

"Picking up the slack as always," Caspere said.

The doors slid open and crew members 1250 to 1257 stepped out onto the platform. They were greeted by two technicians that looked like they'd taken a dip in an oil pool. The shorter of the two extended a filthy hand—no one took it.

"What happened?"

"We passed through the asteroid belt sooner than we thought we would. The mouth wasn't closed in time and a bunch of shit came flying in," said the tech.

"We didn't hear anything," Dane chimed in.

"The desserts. The whole place could have been falling apart and we might not have heard it." Grier turned his attention back on the tech. "So what can we do?"

"Well, two of the capsules went straight into the 'grynder. So, no worries there. However, there are still two more that crashed into the stomach walls—we lost at least dozen of our own. Your job is to retrieve the wreckage for us and if there's anything still alive, terminate it."

"Terminate." Dane felt weird saying the word. "

The technician shrugged. "The scout ship for the next feeding location came back, too."

"So?"

"The rumor is everyone on board was dead. There was

a note attached to one of the pilots that read: TURN BACK NOW. This is just a precaution." The tech smiled. "Kinda funny when you think about it, though. There really isn't much they can do to stop us."

***

It wasn't hard for Dane and his two crewmates—Caspere and Sloane—to find the capsule. The vessel had plowed through a side-wall, destroyed several living units, and finally came to a stop embedded in one of the recreation rooms. Sparks erupted intermittently as Dane and the other two crew workers approached the large blue lozenge-shaped pod.

The front of the capsule had been ripped off in the crash. Dane looked down to see an empty pilot's seat. A bag of weapons sat crumpled to the side. Red dotted the interior wall. Dane's eyes moved from the blood to the leftover bag of goodies. Whoever had been riding in this thing had probably been tossed from it—if they were lucky they died on impact.

He looked through the tunnel of destruction it had made, wondered if maybe one of those multi-colored smears had been the pilot. A small wave of relief washed over Dane. He was fully prepared to kill the intruder, but a part of him was also relieved that today wasn't the day he made the jump from worker to executioner—although, in his heart, Dane knew he would have done it.

"How are we going to get this thing out of here?" Caspere was next to Dane, chewing on the inside of his lip.

"I think we should just drag it and dump it into the 'grynder." Dane pointed to the large hole at the end of the makeshift tunnel.

"Sounds good to me. Sloane, you cool with that?"

23

Sloane, shaggy-haired, and pudgy gave them a thumbs up—he didn't enjoy conversation much. The few times Dane had spoken with him his answers were clipped, one-word responses.

They lifted the pod up, which was fairly light with the three of them hefting it. From the corner of his eye Dane saw a brief flash of light above. He didn't think anything of it until seconds later when Caspere's head disintegrated into a pile of red fluid and skull shrapnel.

Dane and Sloane dropped the capsule. Another flash lit up the space with white light and Sloane pitched backward; a splash of blood hit the ceiling. Dane's heartbeat pulsed in his ears. He told himself to grab one of the guns from the bag in the pod, but couldn't get his feet to move forward. A stream of urine ran down his leg and instead of diving for cover, chasing the shooter, or grabbing a weapon of his own, Dane threw his hands up, and waited to be vaporized.

After a few seconds passed and nothing turned him into a cloud of dust and blood, Dane put his arms down. There were no more flashes. Steam rose from the hole in Sloane's gut. The worker's eyes were wide open, frozen forever in surprise. A few feet away Caspere's headless bulk lay flat on its back, which bothered Dane less. He didn't have the same awful contorted face that Sloane had.

Embarrassment flooded in. This was the second time in less than twenty four hours that Dane had shown fear. He wondered why the halls weren't filled with the sound of the other crewmen. They had to of heard the shots ring out.

He searched exposed ductwork above him. There were spaces in between the floors that left room for workers and air flow. The flash had come from somewhere up and off to the right. He checked for a blood trail, found none, which meant the wound probably wasn't that bad.

It occurred to Dane that he could head back and alert the rest that there was someone hiding out, but did he need to? That would only prove to the rest of his crew that he was a failure, someone the Master couldn't rely on. Besides, the pod only held one person and if they had any ammo left, they would have obliterated him, which meant they had nothing else to defend themselves with—made them an easier target for Dane.

And, maybe, just maybe, he could still redeem himself in the Master's eyes.

Chapter Four

Dane found the woman from the pod in one of the units on the floor above them. From what Dane could gather, she blasted the flooring out, crawled in, killed the occupants inside, and fired down at Dane and the others, while they tried to move the one-person container. It was actually pretty impressive that she had been able to hit two of them from where she was. Had Dane been in the same situation, he would have just turned the blaster on himself.

She held a hand against her side. A dark spot formed, staining the fabric of her black long-sleeved shirt. Chunks of bloody tile lay scattered across the unit floor. Her head was shaved down to stubble. She stared as he hoisted himself up through the hole.

Standing up fully in the unit, he could see the three busted inspector snakes laying in the shower stall. He wasn't familiar with the room's occupant whose head was smashed against the ground despite his chest pointing skyward.

The gun sat limp in her right hand. A small, red light blinked rapidly near the grip. Dane didn't need to be familiar with the weapon to know that it meant the device was empty. He had her at a disadvantage and felt hope rising in the back of his mind. This was it. Redemption had finally come to Dane Shipps, Worker 1255.

He went over how he was going to do it. He could rush back down and snag something from her bag. That would ironic, he thought. Killed with the same instruments she intended to hurt them with. But that would draw this out longer than need be. She might pass away during that time and Dane wanted to make sure the Master knew he dealt the deathblow.

Are you sure you want to do this?

Of course I do. This is what we do. By his grace, I am alive. And by his grace, we survive.

Dane brought the images of Sloane and Casper to mind, reminded himself that this woman had killed two of his longtime crew members. This woman was a stranger. He owed her nothing. Her and the other terrorists had come here to destroy them and failed. Now, they had to deal with the consequences and feed the machine.

Dane crouched in front of her. Her right arm sprung up, clutching a shard of tile. He grabbed her wrist, twisted until the amateur dagger clattered to the floor. He let his hand slide over her throat, squeezed, until her eyes bugged out like two pools of ice.

"Wai...wait..."

Dane kept his grip firm. He couldn't let go. This was the moment where he made up for his previous failings. When he left this room the Master would pardon him of his past sins and accept him back into the fold.

He didn't see the woman's thumb until it was shoving his eyeball further into his skull. She hooked her other hand onto his face, dug chunks of flesh from his cheek. His grip loosened just for a moment, but it was all she needed. The woman caught his wrist, brought it back until the tendons popped.

She threw herself at him and Dane found himself on his back. The woman straddled him, picked up gun and brought it across his face three times.

"I told you to wait," she said. "There was something I wanted to say."

Dane stared up at the woman that has bested him. Her

eyes were intense. There was no doubt in Dane's mind that she would reload and blow his face off without hesitation. Blood trickled into his eye-socket. He wiped it away and became painfully aware of how unprepared he was. This should have been easy, though. The fate of the entire ship was dependent on the death of this woman, and he couldn't even do that right.

Dane looked up at the cold grey ceiling. "I'm going to die."

The woman studied him. Dane wondered how far her and her friends had come and how they knew where King Space Void would be—never had there been a breach in the system and Dane was intrigued by how they accomplished such a feat.

"Will you listen to me now?"

Dane waited a moment before responding. He wished that Grier would come busting through the wall. His co-worker had always been the most violent of the pair. Dane realized that he wasn't a death-dealer, though he wanted to be. He was the cleanup guy; his job was to wipe the messes away and repair broken machinery, not chop off heads. And he certainly had not been prepared to be face-to-face with a woman like the one pinning him to the floor.

Fresh tears and blood ran down Dane's face. The urge to please the Master now completely flushed from his system.

"What do you have to say?"

"I want to show you something," she said.

Then she leaned down and kissed him.

***

At first it was no different than the kisses he shared with partners in the Aphrodite. Her tongue probed and danced with his. She tasted of salt and oil, but that wasn't enough to deter the pleasure that enticed Dane's groin. Something pinched his tongue. Iron leaked into his mouth. His heart thumped against his breastbone like a trapped prisoner. Her lips turned to hot mush as they fused to his.

Dane's eyes opened. The blue eyes he had found breathtaking were gone. Now replaced by two dark pits and in the center a swirling mass of what looked like galaxies.

"I want to show you what you're people are responsible for." Her voice slithered into his head. His brain worked feverishly to make sense of it, but gave up when he felt her tongue glide into his nasal track to lap at his brain.

Dane's mind ruptured. Thousands of images burst across his line of vision. He saw worlds on fire. Civilizations and creatures sprinting through forests to seek refuge from the monstrous eyes of the King Space Void as it loomed on the horizon, eyes ablaze like supernovas.

This was the first time Dane had seen the face of his God. It was nothing like the stories or how he envisioned it. The flesh of King Space Void's face was purple and pocked with black blemishes. More of King Space Void came into view, blotting out the sun. Its mouth was agape showing off its massive steel teeth.

In the vision he saw other things, too, hidden in the secret spaces of the universe. Gaunt humanoid figures wandered an astral plane, while they watched King Space Void tear through the Galaxy, snacking on everything in its path. Screams and an amalgam of voices threaded together to create an indecipherable wail in Dane's ears. Then, as the noise reached its peak, there was a sudden silence. Dane was floating through bluish clouds down onto a lush pink surface.

Standing in front of him was the woman that had latched onto his face. She wore a red flowing gown. To his left was a red sea with several other pads of land floating on its surface. The sky above was a blue-grey sketch. Dane felt his equilibrium shift as the land beneath his feet shifted among the waves.

"This is my planet," the woman said.

"Why are you showing this to me?"

"So you can see what your ship is destroying."

"We're not destroying. We're surviving. We feed the machine, so that we can make it to the Edge."

The woman grinned with perfect pearls. The sight made him embarrassed of his cracked and yellow tombstone chompers.

"The edge is a myth. It doesn't exist on any of the planes. It's an illusion, a goal that will never be reached. No matter how far your death machine travels. You will never make it because it's fantasy."

"Bullshit. The Master would never lie to us. By his grace I am alive, and by his grace I will survive."

"Have you ever been to the other parts of the ship?"

"I've had no reason to," Dane said.

"Then you know nothing about the space in which you live."

"I know that the Master watches over us," Dane said.

"He watches over you as if you were assets, but there are things aboard this ship that have no right being here."

"Yeah, like you and your friends?"

"We're doing what needs to be done. To preserve this world and the few remaining ones like it."

Flowers sprouted from the ground and expelled glowing balls the size of marbles. When they reached the water they each created their own light. The sea turned from red to fish-belly blue.

Dane walked to the edge. In the water he could see the

formation of life take place in the form of multi-eyed fish, some small, and others the size of small people.

"This is one of the last places that can create life," she said. "We cannot allow you to continue to do this. And even if we did, you will not survive much longer."

"Who's we?"

"The gods that rightfully own this universe."

"The Master is a god. And King Space Void is my home and you won't take that away from me!"

Dane was tired of hearing his assaulter speak. He advanced, but the woman laughed, and the ground split before him. He glimpsed those cold blue eyes as he fell to the center of the unknown woman's planet. Lava roiled underneath, eager to strip the bones from Dane's skin.

Before he hit the bottom, Dane's eyes snapped open. The woman was still perched on his chest like a malignant rock. Her mouth hung loose and bloody, as if it had been stretched out just a bit too far. His lips felt like they'd been skinned and rubbed with a palm full of salt.

"Do you understand what I've shown you?"

In response, Dane jabbed a forefinger into the woman's wound. She wailed and drove her knee into Dane's groin, eliciting a howl of pain. She rolled off and made for the hole in the floor. Bile rising up into his throat, Dane tried to get to his feet. He had to catch her and bring her to the Master himself, but the throbbing that coursed from his testicles up into his lower abdomen kept him pinned.

The woman disappeared from the room. Underneath him, Dane heard her running as fast as she could away from the crash site.

Two strikes in one night, Dane thought to himself.

This wasn't going to end well.

Chapter Five

Dane limped out to a walkway crowded with workers from the gut.

Mercy, he thought. *I hope the Master has mercy on me.*

A cage dangled above the pit below. Despite how many people had stepped out to witness the execution, the entire shaft was quiet, except for the rubber creak of the wire holding the cage. Inside the cage was the other terrorist, the one that Grier and his crew had effectively caught and brought back to the Master like dutiful hounds.

"There is poison in our system," The Master's voice bellowed from the wall speakers. "Our lives have been disrupted. These individuals don't think you deserve a happy, peaceful journey to the Edge."

The prisoner yelled. Dane couldn't tell whether he was cursing them all to a fiery death or begging for his life. Either way, the man was passionate about it. Spittle flung from his mouth and the tendons in his neck bulged as he raged and jabbed his fingers at them

"Fucker thought he could get the best of us." Grier slapped Dane on the shoulder. "Too bad there was nothing left of your kill, bud. How'd you take her out again?"

"One of their weapons. Set it to vaporize."

Dane didn't want his failure to be broadcast across the entire gut. It was bad enough that Dane stood there, shoulders slumped like a scolded child. If he was trying to convince everyone that his story about killing the woman was true, he was doing a terrible job. Still, there was a sliver of hope that the Master would take pity on him. Someone so wise would understand that it wasn't Dane's fault. No way could he have anticipated the kind of tricks she'd pulled on him.

"Shame about Sloane and Caspere, too."

"They were good guys," Dane said.

Grier's grip tightened on Dane's bony shoulder. "Good weapon, huh? Disintegrates everything. Where is it?"

Dane's back tightened. Grier was intimidating, but he wasn't good at hiding his intent. Suspicion oozed from the sound of his voice. Dane bit down on the inside of his lip; did hst to look detached and not give away anything.

"Tossed it."

Dane was going to say something about being disappointed. That the lack of an opportunity to experience a kill up close and personal was something he wanted to see, but before he could get the words out the man in the cage went silent.

"Intruder," the Master asked. "Are you responsible for the deaths of those aboard our scout ship?"

The captive's response was to laugh. A dry hack that rose in pitch until it hit a crescendo of mania. It went on for several moments before he stopped and asked the Master, "What do you think?"

Suddenly the captive's body began to ripple, like there were bubbles forming just underneath the surface of his skin. Eyelids split and dripped down the front of his cheeks to accommodate his eyeballs, inflating till they burst like stomped water balloons.

The man screamed and sis throat bulged like it were hiding a fist. Then came the wet sound of tearing as his skin split and revealed flesh stained green.

This bodily deconstruction went on for a few more moments. Every atom in the captive's body gave up. Several spots on his body erupted like squeezed boils until nothing was left, but a human puddle. Thick drops of melted-man spilled from inside the cage and plummeted down into the tooth-ringed may of the Whahchugrynder.

Dane saw himself falling; flung from the balcony and forgotten, replaced within weeks by another worker. He desperately wanted to go back to earlier in the day; when he was enjoying himself in the throes of ecstasy in the Aphrodite, careless and happy. Now he was stuck with needling fear of going back to his room to face the Master.

He watched the spectacle for a little longer. The Whahchugrynder lapped up the liquefied man, coiling around itself, and dragging its barbed tongue along the walls of the shaft. It had no eyes, but a mouth like busted garbage disposal. Its body a ribbed tube that could intake anything it turn into useful energy. It was mindless. It was hungry. And it eagerly awaited the arrival of its newest tenant.

Dane realized in that moment, watching the creature below swirl in its own brown and green fluids, that he didn't want to die. He would explain himself. Somehow convince the Master that he was worth saving. Dane would agree to take on extra duties even if it meant no sleep and took a toll on his body.

He would make a case for himself.

And hope that the Master understood.

Chapter Six

Dane threw his clothes to the floor.

Fuck it, he thought. If the inspector snakes wanted to screen him so be it. He had done his best to do his job, and to do it well; to punish him in such a way didn't seem fair considering how hard he had worked all his life. The woman had shown King Space Void to him as a monstrous figure, an engine of death, waging genocide across the entire universe. She wanted Dane to see the Master as compassionless and power hungry. What she didn't realize, was all they wanted was to reach the Edge where they could finally have peace.

The dying man's laugh nagged at his brain. Why had he died in such a horrible way? Maybe that had been the plan all along? Infiltrate and infect, maybe. There certainly wasn't a way for them to escape once inside King Space Void. Dane figured they knew that coming in, though, and from his experience, they didn't seem like the fearful type. When he found the woman she hadn't cried out or tried to escape—she attacked *him*.

The things she had shown him. The things she said to him. Yes, King Space Void had caused a lot of destruction, but it was in order to survive. If those civilizations were faced with the same dilemma, then they would have made the same choices. He understood their fear as King Space Void loomed above them, but there was nothing he could do to change their course of action.

How much do you know about your own ship, she had asked him.

The question offended Dane. It inferred he had no knowledge about his own people, which was bullshit; he knew his world well. It may have been true, that Dane had not been anywhere but the gut, but his faith assured him that he was not alone in his service of the Master.

Naked, Dane stepped into the shower stall, punched in the code for the stream of water to eject. The lights above blinked on and the floor vibrated; the telltale sound of an oncoming inspection.

Good, Dane thought. *I will confess what I have to confess and the Master will understand. He may be strict, but he is also forgiving.*

"Master," Dane said.

The Inspector Snakes rose like steel cobras ready to strike.

"I want to speak to the Master," Dane said. "There's no need for an inspection. I want to explain my failures and ask for forgiveness."

No answer. The snakes hovered, waiting for orders.

Dane's heartbeat quickened. This was it; the moment of absolution. His mind told him to run; to get out of the shower stall at that very moment. He pushed the thought away. The Master wouldn't have respect for someone that would turn and run, but Dane was sure that this bold display of obedience and willingness to admit failure, would win him some favor—would let the Master know that this was a one-off, that Dane was still dedicated to the cause; a reliable citizen.

The sad fact is, he thought. *No one can rely on you. Your mind is built to question things even if you don't want to admit it. You can push them away or attempt to forget, but the truth is, you wanted to reach out and touch the woman, but not in a harmful way; a loving way; a way that would comfort her. When it comes down to it, you don't want to be as blind as the rest.*

No sound came from the speakers. It was just Dane and the inspector snakes. The realization that the Master was not going to hear him out became more and more apparent as the seconds ticked by—this wasn't an inspection, it was Dane's punishment.

The sound of familiar whirring filled the room. Dane felt the greased up metal coils slither around his body, eager to reveal his secrets. Tremors rippled through his stomach, and he felt the lower snake slide toward his back-end.

The first inspector snake unfurled with petals of pointed steel, darted forward, bounced off Dane's closed mouth, leaving gashes. His hand shot out to grab the second snake that desperately tried to dig itself into his rectum. Muscles burning, Dane pulled it around in front of him and fell down hard on the floor to block off at least one of his orifices.

The first snake made another pass at Dane's face, took a chunk of his temple, as he moved to the side. The third snake wrapped itself around his throat, tightened across his windpipe. Pain exploded in Dane's hand as blades erupted from the body of the snake, digging deep into the flesh of his right hand. Dribbles of red ran down his forearm.

He was getting it from all sides. The snakes weren't interested in his secrets, but instead were settling for doing as much damage to his body as possible. They lashed out. His chest, face, and legs wept.

Specks of dust populated his vision. The pressure on his throat tightened. Fire ran through his chest. He didn't know why, but as darkness bled into his vision, when his anger should have flared up the most at the woman he failed to kill, Dane felt only sadness and regret. He was doomed from the moment that arm scared him earlier that day. Deep down, Dane knew he was never meant to be a killer—if that had been ingrained in the unique DNA of who he was, he wouldn't be there wrestling with snakes.

Two of the snakes stopped lashing out at him, and instead took to entwining his arms and legs, shredding flesh as they went. He cried out as the one wrapped on his left arm hit a snag, as if the bone were stronger than the blades. He tried to move; tried to get into an angle where he could pull himself free, but his palms slipped on the blood-slick tile.

Dane gnashed his teeth. He'd go out screaming if that was the case. A voice in the back of his head hollered that he'd been betrayed and deep down, Dane knew that was the truth. He'd been deceived by the Lord above, who in reality, didn't care if Dane bled to death in his shower stall, alone and mangled.

Dane didn't want to admit it, but the woman was right. He was a cog, a piston in a death machine. He was only good for as long as he kept up his expected function. The world she had shown him flashed before his eyes. Beautiful. Serene. A place where all life and beauty sprung from. It was a whole new world, which made Dane realize something else. He'd never been to any of the other floors aboard the ship; didn't really know what they held. It had been steel shafts, carnivorous worms, and other workers his whole life. For all he knew, the Master was dead and someone else was pulling strings.

A mental dam had been broken. Questions flooded in that he'd never considered before. What was it like at the top? What did the other floors hold? And Why were there so many sealed off areas in the gut?

You're never gonna know, said the voice in his head. *This is the end of the journey for you Dane Shipps.*

…and then the power went out.

Chapter Seven

The inspector snakes fell limp.

Dane lay in the fetal position, snared by metal whips. He waited for the power to come back and the snakes to resume their assault. Outages were rare, but when they did happen, they only lasted a few minutes at most.

There wasn't an inch of Dane's skin didn't feel as if it had been dragged down a road of broken glass. His pulse thumped in his head. He slowly opened his eyes. The room was black. The medical kit was underneath the steel sing a few feet away, but even that was too far.

The darkness and silence drew on for a long time before it hit him.

He pushed himself up against the stall wall, amazed that he hadn't thought of it sooner. Pain blossomed as his back kissed the tile. The human sludge that their prisoner had turned into wasn't some biological flub, it was a defense mechanism. Whether it was their plan all along or a plan B he didn't know, but he was certain that right now the goo that had dripped from the cage had infected the 'grynder worm.

Dane didn't need a more obvious sign than the power outage. The people that had infiltrated King Space Void weren't stupid; they were prepared. Unlike the Master who relied on fear and arrogance to make a point, these people worked together to achieve a goal. Whatever doubts he had about remaining loyal to the Master fled his mind. The thought of no longer crawling through hot ducts and working every muscle till it burned seemed like a dream he didn't know he wanted. Now the fantasy had the potential to become a reality.

Submit and die. Run and maybe die. These were Dane's only choices.

It wasn't a hard decision. He just had to get to the med-kit and do what he could. After, he'd find the woman aboard King Space Void, tell her that he wanted to join her cause.

"Damn, you're one fucked up lapdog," said a voice in the dark.

***

The shower door fell open. Dane was greeted by the woman. In the dark her eyes glinted yellow-green.

"I take it you and your God had a disagreement."

Dane sighed. He wasn't in the mood to be chastised again. The Master's attempt to take his life was enough for a lifetime.

Her knees popped as she crouched down. The scent of vanilla and copper rolled off her. In an odd way, Dane felt comforted by her presence. It gave him a sliver of hope that he might make it out this alive.

"Why'd you come back?"

"Because," she said, "I think that you can help me save what's left of this universe."

"I'm not a fighter. I think I've proven that much so far."

The woman's laugh was dry and humorless. "No, you're not, but that doesn't mean you can't help."

"What can I do? The Master controls everything."

The woman shook her head like a disappointed mother, sighed.

"You really don't know much about your own world, do you?"

"I know that my entire life has been in service of someone that doesn't give a damn about me. That's what I know."

"The woman bit her lip. That's not the only thing you'll come to know, if you decide to help me. Let's take care of those wounds"

"What about..." Dane pointed at where the gash in the woman's stomach used to be. A square of gauze covered it.

"I'm good as new," she said. "You, on the other hand, look like shit."

"Thanks for telling me...again."

The woman reached into her pack, threw a handful of what looked like dust into the air. Particles exploded like tiny blue fireworks, illuminating the room in translucent light. She grimaced at his cut up body.

Dane tried to force a smile, but the pain corkscrewed from the opening in his cheek and up into his temple. She crouched down and began removing the defunct snakes from his body, which took longer than expected, and was accompanied by Dane's one man show of whimpering.

While she worked on him, Dane tried to play the events of the last few hours over in his mind. His emotions were a melting pot. He knew he had failed the lord above, but his intentions to do well were pure. At the time, Dane had every intention of killing this woman. Now, though, after the worlds she had shown him, and the natural beauty of her planet, a small voice told him to question the thing's he had learned. In the span of a few minutes, this woman hadn't just talked to him about a better life; she had shown him what a better life looked like, which was more than the Master had ever done. He'd only spoken of the Edge, but provided no tangible evidence of its existence.

For the first time in his life, Dane began to doubt the Master's plan.

She set the snakes down to the side, pulled a small hammer-like object from a pack next to her, and pounded the metal bodies to dust. She dropped the hammer and held up a small hand torch and tube full of liquid chalk.

"Wait a minute," Dane said. "I've seen what you're capable of? Can't you just snap your fingers and patch me up?"

"No, sometimes simple is best."

"What's your name," Dane asked, hoping to stall a little longer before she worked him over.

"Scarlet. Now be quiet."

He tried to say his name, but her hand muffled the words, and the real screaming started.

Chapter Eight

When Scarlet finished patching Dane up, he was surprised that the pure shock and adrenaline pumping through his body hadn't shut his heart down. The anesthetic worked faster than expected; within moments the dull throb that coursed through his entire body began to subside. He hoped that it wasn't the type of stuff that wore off after a while; there was no way he could sit through that again.

"I have to tell you something," Dane said.

"What?" Scarlet slung the bag over her shoulder.

Dane's face turned red with embarrassment; his eyes moved downward. "Well, I've never even seen the Master before, and, if to be honest, I don't know how to get up there. All the doors are sealed. The shaft only opens up when something triggers the sensors in the mouth to get the doors rolling."

"Okay, so?"

"Well, what's your plan?"

Scarlet didn't appear bothered by Dane's revelation or the obstacles before them. "Easy, we just keep moving up. When a door doesn't open, we make our own door."

***

They walked out onto the walkway where hours earlier Dane had watched Scarlet's partner turn into a human stew right before his eyes. The area was deserted. Various sections of King Space Void's internal machinery were still working, casting a dull green light on the otherwise dark pit below them. So the infection hadn't shut everything down, but it had caused some major damage. The 'grynder wasn't curling over itself, aching for its next meal, but instead was a floating mass of fleshy tubing.

A belched echoed through the portholes built into the shaft. Dane heard a rumbling sound similar to rushing water. Black waves spilled forth and carried with them chunks of swirling brown masses. The ripe smell of waste made them both gag.

"Good people of King Space Void."

"Shit…"

"Your freedom and livelihoods are in danger. There are people who do not want you to be happy. You want to be happy don't you? To make it to the Edge we have to feed the machine with what it needs to survive."

Another belch and a waterfall of muck ran from a porthole directly above them.

The entire ship rumbled. Multi-colored lights winked on throughout the ship as King Space Void roared back to life before them. In the full light, Dane could see cancerous lines running from the waters below and up across the surface of the walls like malignant vines.

"There is poison in our system," said the Master.

On the other side of the shaft, Dane watched Grier step out from one of the hallways. There was no anger on the crewman's face. Only a simple look of determination that made Dane's arms erupt in gooseflesh; if Grier got a hold of him, Dane wasn't so sure he could hold on own in a fight.

"Feed the machine," King Space Void bellowed. "And survive."

Footsteps rang out from all directions. Dozens of people stepped out onto the three-tiered walkways, carrying pipes and chains. Some had removed the skin from their arms to show off the metal rods and struts that served as skeletal structure, which Dane had never seen before.

Scarlet dropped the bag, pulled a stubby weapon from it, and blew a hole in the walkway at their feet. She gripped Dane by the shirt, dragged him down to the next floor before he had a chance to protest.

His knee rang out as they landed.

"Which way?!"

Dane turned right and headed back to the Room of Aphrodite. When they burst into the room, he half-expected to be greeted by a pack of nude murderers eager to dismantle them and lob their body parts into the grinder. Instead they walked in on a colossal orgy that even made Dane stop and admire the sheer ferocity of the monolithic display of coupling.

Someone had opened the spirit boxes, too. They lay open, empty of their contents. Dane's navigate through the rolling mountain of flesh. It was easy to spot whom had become vessels. They floated above the ground, blue light spilled from their mouths and eyes, washing over the bodies before them.

Several of the partiers withdrew from their partners, knelt before the possessed bodies. Their heads were brought to glowing labia and cocks where they licked and sucked like water-deprived desert dwellers. The possessed leaned their heads back until it sagged between their shoulders. Hijacked fingers prodded and pulled on stomach flesh until it split down the middle.

Dane looked on with a mixture of fear and curiosity as the possessed opened their bodies to the entire room. The room filled with cries for help intermingled with pleas to join the ranks of the damned that had taken residence inside the floating hosts. Some crawled forward on bruised knees, eager to join the swirling mass of souls inside.

Three shots rang out in succession. Ectoplasm and grey matter showered those closest to the possessed as they all fell lifeless to the floor of the Aphrodite. Those that had been watching went back to rutting on the floor, while a few still tried to force themselves into the torsos of their deceased counterparts.

In the middle of the room, standing on a table above the tangle of sweaty bodies, was a man Dane had never seen before. Wisps of smoke trailed from the barrel of the contraption in his hand. Shaggy grey hair rolled out from under the green fedora he wore. The ragged coat tails of his jacket bobbed as the man gestured wildly to the people before him.

"The world you live in is a joke! There is no greater plan or life in store for any of you! You all live to serve something more than you'll ever be. So, enjoy this break that you are being given. Take advantage of not only the pleasure you are feeling, but notice the elation your body feels after it has reached its climax! This is as good as it gets, my friend! Trust me. I've seen what this universe harbors, and let me tell you good people of this slave dimension, there is nothing nice out there in the big, black beyond. These are the moments you should live for!"

The moans reached an intense pitch, ranging from high wails to trombonesque grunts. Fedora Man held his arms out wide and turned around. His plum-colored vest was soaked. When he saw Dane and Scarlet he smiled, mouth too small for so many teeth.

"Greetings, friends! Might I ask that you take your clothes off if you are going to join us?"

"I've never seen you before," Dane said. "What are you

doing here?"

"That's because I've never had the opportunity to visit this part of the glorious dimension we all share."

"It's just a ship," Dane said.

"Ship. Dimension. Whatever you want to call it, the truth is there are whole civilizations living on the damnable thing, and up until recently, there have been areas that were previously off limits." Fedora Man pulled his bowtie loose, tucked it neatly into the pocket of his jacket, and started on the buttons. "Now, though, there are more doors open, and some of us are free to roam, do as we please."

Fedora Man parted the mid-section of his silk shirt. Attached to his abdomen were three elephant trunks grew from his mid-section.

"Besides, your Master has been using the milk from my people to create a lot of what you're ingesting. I thought it was time to see what the entire hubbub was about. You!" Fedora Man snapped his fingers and pointed to two people frantically humping at the base of the table. Their eyes were glassy, but they stood. Fedora Man cupped the back of their heads, brought their mouths to his appendages.

The naked man and woman suckled like children. Milk spilled from between their lips, dripped to the floor. Fedora Man threw his head back and laughed, cupped their heads guided them into a smooth rhythm.

"Take all that you can now, little zombies. The wells are running dry. Transcend with me!"

Fedora Man pushed them away. Sadness filled their eyes, but they retreated like wounded dogs when Fedora Man held his hand up, ready to bring it across their mouths. This went on for a few more moments with Fedora Man feeding a few lucky workers and then casting them back into the pile.

Three nude men rounded the side the pile of bodies,

stopped in front of Dane and Scarlet.

"Hey, Dane, come join us."

Sweat dribbled down their naked chests. Any other time Dane would have invited himself to lick those salty dribbles off. With Scarlet next to him, though, and the realization that the drugs and the sex were tools used to manipulate them, Dane just felt sad for his three friends that all stood eagerly and erect before him. Fedora Man looked amused at Dane's display of hesitation.

"Let's get out of here," Scarlet said. "We need to be going up anyway."

"I don't think that is best of ideas," Fedora Man said.

They turned in time to see Grier stride into the Aphrodite, carrying no weapons, just a smug smile. Dane had seen that grin a thousand times before. Grier only got it when he was given a job that he was overqualified for. A handful of people stood behind him, all ready to tear Dane and Scarlet limb from limb in service of the Master.

"I'm gonna have to stop you right there. The Master wants to see you fed to the 'grynder. So, if you please. Come with us." Grier gestured toward the door.

The three naked men moved around Scarlet and Dane.

"Hey, Grier. Shelley. Chris. Dane and his new friend don't want to join us. What about you guys?"

"Fuck off, Todd." Dane shoved the guy backward.

The second naked man slid behind Grier, rubbed his shoulders. "It's so much better with you, buddy."

The man behind him would have nibbled Grier's neck had the scarred crewman not slammed the back of skull into his unwanted lover's nose. Twin rivulets of blood ran down his bare chest as he stumbled back and fell onto his ass.

"Oh, I love it!" Fedora Man cried out.

To Dane's surprise Todd didn't strike out. He sat on the

floor, smiled up at Grier with blood-streaked teeth. Reaching out and giggling like a young man who knows he's being bad, Todd gripped the cuff of Grier's pants. "Let's get these off."

Grier drove his fist downward. Teeth skittered across the metal floor. Dane tried not to look at Todd's pulsing erection. The abuse was getting him off, not pulling him out of the fog. The other two guys grappled with Grier's posse.

Grier turned to Dane. "Let's go, Shipps. The ship is sick and you need to help fight the infection. Take this as your opportunity to atone. Be a good dog."

"You're a dog, too, my friend."

Dane wanted to explain to Grier everything he had come to terms with in the last hour. That they were being spoonfed lies. They knew nothing about King Space Void other than what they were told. He didn't get the chance though because before Dane could utter the words the Fedora Man cleared his throat.

"Excuse me! Yes, all of you that just joined us, listen to what I have to say." Fedora Man looked over and winked at Dane and Scarlet. "I know this may be a tumultuous time for you, but trust me, I can solve your problems."

Fedora Man had to shout over the grunts and screams of the bodies surrounding them.

"Don't you want these two poor souls to enjoy themselves," Fedora Man pointed to Dane and Scarlet. "... before they must succumb?"

Grier shook his head. "I don't know who you are, but you don't belong here."

Fedora Man jumped down from the table, stepped through the maze of people. He stopped in front Grier and smiled. "Oh, but I do. What you've been smoking and eating down here...half of that belongs to me."

Grier's fist crashed into the Fedora Man's cheek. An eyeball jumped from its socket. The showman stumbled backward, hand clutched to his face. When he took his hand away, Dane saw that a flat green landscape had been hiding behind Fedora Man's faux face.

"Well that's disappointing," Fedora Man said. "I worked hard on that mask, but I suppose I should've seen it coming."

Fedora Man sauntered back to the table, looked to Dane and Scarlet, said, "You might want to take a few steps back."

Scarlet and Dane pressed themselves against the far wall. Fedora Man tugged lightly on the three trunks that protruded from his torso. After a moment they curved upward, rigid and dripping with milk. Fedora Man took a deep breath and then exhaled. Gouts of white fluid sprayed into the air, coating the crew members fucking on the floor.

Grier jumped back a few feet, shoving two other crew members in front of him.

Fedora Man spun on his heel, hosing everyone down. When his twirl came to a close , Fedora Man jumped down from the table. He knelt by the closest person, whispered something, and then drove a fist up into the man's chest. The man leapt upon his partner, dug his teeth into her shoulder. Her head snapped back in ecstasy as she ground herself harder against the man's crotch. With a free hand she grabbed her lover's wrist, guided his hand to her mouth, and began nibbling the flesh from his fingers.

Dane's mind worked to take in the scene before him. Neither of the parties appeared bothered by the mutual bodily humiliation. The woman detached herself from the man, turned and shoved him to the ground. She mounted him, dug her nails into the meat of his chest, and began to pull the skin in opposite directions, stretching it like tan taffy.

The fever spread. Those that had been worshipping the

possessed began pulling strips of skin from the vacant body and feeding one another. Two people scrambled over to the last of spirit boxes, pried it open. The occupant burst from inside it's prison, floated above them, muttering the word "slaves" over and over. Fedora Man threaded his way through the blood and sex. When he reached Dane and Scarlet, he reached out and put his hands on both their shoulders.

"We should get out of here," Fedora Man said.

"Why do you want to help us," Scarlet asked.

"You're going upstairs to see the big guy, right? Well, there are some things I'd like answered, too. Let's get out of here, though. Unless you all want to die in a really sexy, fun way."

"And who are you," Dane asked.

"My name is Lee," Fedora Man said. "Now, if we could, please get out of here before someone rips my dick off. I rather like where it's at."

They headed for the front door of the Aphrodite, Scarlet leading the way. From across the room, Grier tried to wade through the sea of flesh, but an arm dragged him down. He fell across a group of nude men and women that met the scarred worker with eager arms and mouths. Dane averted his eyes. Squeals and screams that didn't contain a hint of lust erupted, followed by the sound of crushing bones and shredded flesh.

The entity from the spirit box began to lose pieces of its anatomy. Chunks of its glowing chest dropped into top of sweat-slick heads, while its arms and legs dripped into the mouths of the eager workers below it. They swallowed more and more of the apparition until finally there was nothing left of it, but a glowing shred of it.

A woman snatched final chunk of ghost from the air, gobbled it up. Two of the newly possessed, both men, began to emit the same kind of light that the earlier ones had, only instead of opening themselves up like human portals they staggered toward each other, arms outstretched. They embraced one another and almost instantaneously the tops of their skulls split open, as if assaulted by a large axe. Gouts of blood and ectoplasm hit the ceiling of the Aphrodite.

The skinnier of the two scooped the others brain from its bone-bowl, devoured it, while the empty-headed man stood watching the scene unfold with passivity. The other possessed sauntered up behind the vacant vessel. None of the crew members appeared bothered by what was happening. They were lost in their own passions. Lana from Dane's own crew was straddled atop one of King Space Void's engineers. Where her body wasn't streaked with blood, it was covered in a white and blue crust. Her hands gripped Kirk's upper and lower jaw, pulling until the sound of splintered tendons could be faintly heard over the cacophony of fucking and torture.

"Need better flesh," the skinny man said.

Dane didn't need anyone to tell him that the possessed were all sharing the same conscious. They began pulling each other's limbs away. Eyes and ears disappeared from their naked bodies, so that the skinny, more authoritative of the bunch could try on new body parts as if he were at a grotesque fashion show.

Scarlet dragged him to the door. By the time Dane looked back it was impossible to see where Grier might be, but he could tell that the rest of the party had fallen into the violence, happily breaking bones and swallowing gobs of meat from each other. He saw Athena suck an eyeball from the head of another worker, while Todd stood before two people biting pieces of flesh from his body; face swathed in pleasure, Todd hung his head back howled.

The howl followed them out of the Aphrodite and rang on in Dane's ears for long after.

Chapter Nine

The floor was packed with people eager to knock all three of them into the 'grynder's maw. None had the courage, though, to step forward when Scarlet aimed the barrel of her pistol at them. They stared wide-eyed at Lee whose mask hung down the right side of his face. For the first time Dane noticed how hollow the citizens' eyes were. There was only one thing on their minds: appease the Master. Paper thin skin stretched over loyal, but dreary faces. All of them would gladly die for the cause, but there was an inherent fear built into them when faced with the unknown.

The man closest to them stepped forward, hammer in hand. Scarlet pulled the trigger, blew a fist-sized hole into his chest. She shot three citizens in the front to get her point across. Like Dane, most of the workers hadn't seen real bloodshed. Several doubled-over to expel the contents of their stomachs; others attempted to look stoic.

However, no one stepped forward after their comrades were killed. They let the three inch forward and made a path for them to a steel ladder set into the wall, at the end of which was a small foyer that led to a single door.

"How are we going to…"

Scarlet blasted the door to splinters, looked at Dane. "Open the door?"

Dane smiled.

***

When the debris to the next room cleared, Dane hadn't known what to expect. This was his first step beyond the walls of his life. In reality, it didn't matter what was behind the steel doors; he would have been taken aback by anything.

The floor was made of cogs bordered by pistons that ratcheted back and forth, a moving walkway. They hopped from cog to interlocking cog until they made it to a flat escalator. The walls were warped and the color of rusted iron.

"Not much for style here, are they?" Lee said.

"It smells like blood," Scarlet said.

Dane sucked in a lungful of air through his nostrils. She was right. The entire place had a copper tang to it. He was about to make a comment that the walking escalator stopped in a dead end, but then came the booming sound of a huge tumbler lock being released underneath them.

The wall in front of them rose to unveil a factory. Obscenely large metal spires rose high into the air hacking out plumes of black oil-smoke. Mangled bodies fell from a drain embedded into the side of a steel wall and hit the blood-stained belt that wound like a maze on the factory's dirt-packed floor. On every side of the belt were workers, half-machine, and half-human. They yanked pieces of the deposited bodies apart, and replaced whatever had been removed with a bionic replacement.

Dane followed one body from the start. He couldn't discern the gender as it was missing its genitalia. An engine-sized hole had been blown through the chest and its right arm was missing, a shredded stump sat just below the shoulder.

The first worker, head molded from a steel beams, held up its right arm, which ended in a circular saw. It cleared away the threads of meat. Satisfied with its work, it walked back to a box spilling over with cables, and jammed a fistful of them into the body's flesh and down the line it went. Two more workers hefted a small box affixed with dials and an air vent into the chest cavity. The final stop required only one worker to slide a cable into the port set in the center. Power surged into the new heart. The cables went wild, striking out at anything close with its electrified blue tips.

One of the robotic technicians walked to a long chain that hung from the wall, pulled on it. A horn blared across the space. All the technicians dropped what they were doing and rose their hands into the air, cheered. The sound of beeping horns grew in tandem with the self-aggrandizing applause.

A woman, head adorner by swirls of blue cotton candy hair, passed by them carrying a clipboard. Dane noticed a small limp in her step, but was captivated by the thin stockings she wore. Screws and nails pierced the thin flesh of her ears and rattled as she moved away from them.

The deeper they went into the factory, the more Dane could see how productive and efficient the workers were. Corpses fell, got repaired, and revived. His left arm tingled, while he watched the bodies get repaired and sent off to another section.

Above them, imbedded into the face of the wall was a monstrous head, carved from different types of steel. The cheeks looked like sheet metal welded to rebar to give it structure and angles. Copper wiring was strung around the spark plugs jutting from where there should have been a gum line, but was nothing more than more jumbles of wire.

Gasoline-induced infernos blazed in the Machine God's eye sockets. With an unnerving ease, the head titled down. Dane felt the heat wash over them. Lee pulled the fedora over his face. Scarlet didn't seemed bothered. For a moment he feared that the monstrous head would lean down and devour them, but it spoke in a friendly tone.

"Visitors," the machine-god bellowed. "Welcome. You have nothing to fear from us."

The Machine God turned its head slightly to the right. "You look very familiar."

"Me?" Dane pointed to himself.

"Yes, I seem to remember your face, but I can't pinpoint from where. Ah, nevermind. It's not important. What can I do for you?"

"We seek safe passage from here to the top of King Space Void."

"What is King Space Void," asked the Machine God.

"King Space Void is the vessel in which your world exists," Scarlet answered.

The Machine God said nothing, mulled this news over, and then said, "You are referring to the Black Gates beyond."

Dane looked beyond the refineries and metal structures that took up a lot of the land. He could make out a sliver of black. He tried to calculate the width of King Space Void, but none of it made sense in relation to where he'd lived out his life. Dizziness set in. This wasn't the world he expected to find. He thought the faces would resemble his; that there would be floor after floor of workers in grey coveralls, bending wrenches and performing maintenance routines. What he saw instead was an entire world, culture, and type of creature that twisted everything he thought he knew into a ball and lobbed it into the void.

Dane's legs wobbled. Compounded with the visions Scarlet had shown him earlier, his brain was trying to rip itself apart in order to reorganize. Nothing fit, though. It was like trying to slam the wrong pieces of a jigsaw puzzle together.

He jumped when Scarlet placed her hand on his shoulder.

"Hey, you all right?"

"Yeah, my head hurts. I'll be fine."

"We're looking to travel upwards," Lee said to the head.

"Behind this wall there is staircase," the Machine God responded. "Go through the junkyard and you'll see it. I promise you a safe passage."

Dane was drawing circles in the dirt with his finger when Scarlet crouched down in front of him. "You ready?"

"I think I'm just going to stay here."

Scarlet's face scrunched. "What do you mean?"

"I don't want to see what's at the top of that staircase. I can barely understand this." Dane gestured at the sentient machines and then pointed at Lee. "And every time I lay my eyes on him and think back to the Aphrodite, I just want to lie down. Why didn't we see someone or something like this sooner? There are worlds beyond the walls and I never even knew it."

"Hey, calm down. "Scarlet did her best to try and sound comforting, but Dane felt like the threads in his mind had come unspooled and were falling in different directions.

"I got this," Lee said.

Lee took Dane's head into his hands. They were oddly soft for someone whose face looked like a smashed lizard with a missing eye. "King Space Void is sick. Whatever Scarlet's partner did, screwed up the anatomy of your Master. Defenses are down and the boss is vulnerable. I've been trying to claw my way down to your end for years, okay? Just remember you're on a machine. Your god abandoned you and you want to know why.

Dane had dug a significant hole in the ground with his finger.

Lee's grip tightened. "What do you want, Dane?"

"Answers." Dane hated how soft and childlike he

sounded.

"That's right. We're not going to find them here, though. So get up and let's go make that son of a bitch confess his sins to us."

Chapter Ten

The staircase was a frozen brass tornado that wound itself up into a red sky. Dust, the color of coal, and buffeted by the wind coated their bodies. After what felt like hours, Dane's knees began to cramp up. Sweat stung his eyes. Scarlet and Lee didn't seem to be as bothered as Dane. Why would they, he thought? The longer Dane spent with the two of them, the more dawned on them that they had one of the most valuable assets one could ask for: experience.

"Doing all right back there," Less asked over his shoulder.

Dane gripped the banister. "I'm not sure I can keep going. I need to rest."

"We're almost there," Scarlet said. Don't let its appearance fool you. This really isn't as far as it appears to be."

"Just for a moment," Dane said and sat.

Lee pulled his fedora off and using it like a bowl to collect the accumulated sweat at the brim, brought it over to Dane, and poured the contents onto his head. It reeked of body odor and grime, but at least it was cooler than the winds batting his face.

From their vantage point, the machine shops and steel spires looked a handful of scattered car parts. Dane wondered if the Master had ever considered using this world to his advantage; surely they could contribute.

An explosion shook the stairs. The steps vibrated. Dane caught himself from sliding off the step he was resting on. A fireball was lobbed into the sky from the same mountain that the Machine God was built into. The sound of screeching metal filled their ears and two of the metal rods toppled, slamming into the factories below.

Dane knew that their presence had brought the Master's wrath to the Machine God's world. They farther they went, the more the Master would destroy just to keep them from reaching the top of God's castle. There was no way they could escape. If they went back now, surrendered, then maybe their deaths would be swift.

He looked up at the rest of the stair case that towered above them. Whatever lay beyond was terrifying to Dane. He didn't know if he could handle the shock of seeing another world unlike his. It would be easier, he thought to himself, to just run back to the Machine God, kneel before his executioner, and accept his fate

Yes, that is what he would do. Following Lee and Scarlet would only ensure that when the Master reached him, Dane's death would only end that much worse.

He pulled himself to his feet, started back down the stairs.

"Where's he going?"

"Dane," Scarlet said. "What're you doing?'

"I can't do this. If I go back, maybe I can die knowing that I pleased the Lord above."

Scarlet grabbed Dane by the collar of his grey coveralls. Her hand scrunched up his face as she forced him to stare directly at the crumbling factories and metal shops. Flecks of ash peppered his face.

"Look at it. If you go down there, it will change nothing. They'll still come after us and your Master will continue destroying every world he comes across. Do you understand?"

More flecks of black debris wafted over Dane's face. He squinted, tears rolled.

"I will throw you off these fucking stairs if that's what you want, but remember this, it won't change anything. Your death will have no impact other than to validate your worst fears…that your God abandoned you. Or worse, never cared in the first place. Come with us, though, and your life will mean something."

Scarlet removed her hand from Dane's mouth.

He followed them to the next level.

Chapter Eleven

The stairs left them at the start of a road that was bordered by torsos staked to six-foot high wooden poles. Vacant eyes watched the road with disinterest. Some were bent sideways, as if trying to acknowledge their deceased counterparts. Dried skin flapped like rice paper in the wind.

A voice called out to them from down the row. Arms flapped in the air like a hitchhiker trying to flag down the last car left in an apocalyptic wasteland.

The three of them walked down the road. The closer they got to the owner of the voice, the more they realized it was one of the staked people. He greeted them with gold-capped teeth that reflected the sun.

"Greetings," said the Staked Man. "Who might you folks be?"

Scarlet explained their situation to the Staked Man, who nodded, scratched his chin and said, "okay" every so often. When she finished, the Staked Man was silent. His eyes moved to each of them.

"I think I might be able to help you, but as you can see," Stake Man gestured toward to the stick affixed to his torso. "Give me a moment. And plug your ears."

They did as instructed. Stake Man put his head back and screamed. The skin underneath his chest bubbled and split open. An arachnid-like creature freed itself from the contents of its host. Its spindly legs dripped brown syrup that pooled on puckered feet. Two bulbous green eyes sat atop its angel-hair-thin antennae. It observed the three travelers before it and then leapt several feet into the air where it burst into a splash of yellow.

"Well," Lee said. "That's one way to get someone's attention."

Dane realized the sight hadn't sent him running back the way they came. He couldn't help but feel intrigued rather than horrified at the rows and rows of corpses. Dane realized, too, that unlike the horrible contorted mess that had been Sloane's face in death, every one of the bodies before them were smiling, as if they'd died happy.

A wagon came barreling down the road. Its wheels bounced off rocks and a plume of dust surrounded the massive black beast that was its driver. When it stopped in front of them, Dane began to think maybe that old gem of running away wasn't such a terrible idea.

The beast dragging the cart sat on four legs of muscle that were thicker and wider than Dane's wiry frame. It had no eyes, only a mouth that dripped saliva. It growled at the three interlopers, but retreated when the sudden crack of a whip subdued the beast.

A wooden slat slid open in the front of the wagon and another one of arachnid-like creatures gazed out at them with pulsing eyes. "Please, get in."

Scarlet moved around the cart, never taking her eyes off the monster tethered to it. The wooden door opened so fast it nearly clipped Scarlet in the head, but she ducked fast and graceful. Dane admired the way she handled herself in any given situation. Her demeanor never faltered; she just took what came at her, and did what needed to be done.

Something strange wormed its way into his mind. Wouldn't it be nice to spend the rest of their days together? They had been through so much, and had so many experiences, that he knew they couldn't just walk away from each other forever. The image of them laughing together and taking walks on the surface of her planet filled him with an unfamiliar joy.

It made him want to continue their journey…no, *mission*, even more.

Inside the wagon were four more of the red spider creatures.

"We apologize that we are not more presentable," said the creature closest to Dane, and then pricked his arm with a curved nail, and swabbed his blood into a small container. It went down the line, doing the same to Scarlet and Lee; the latter of which complained that if it happened again, there'd be "one less fucking spider aboard."

The creature ignored the threat, opened a small chest, and began to deposit their samples into tiny instruments with symbols and numbers Dane had never seen before. The creature then passed around tubed tipped with needles.

The machine ran through a series of data. Fluids from inside the creatures began to pump into three separate jugs. When the creatures finished siphoning their own blood, they poured the contents of the jugs into plastic cups.

Dane was amazed to find his full of water.

"Drink, please," the creature said. "You are our guest."

"Those people on the road. Are you the ones responsible for that?"

"No." The creature's voice was matter-of-fact. "Our Guard Men are there of their own free will. When one comes to the end of their life here, they are free to become one with the soil, or they have the opportunity to stand guard over the land that gave them the lives they wanted."

"Pretty grotesque," Scarlet said.

"Yes, well, you have to understand that our world is susceptible to infiltration on a regular basis. We have to make it known that Seyveria is not welcoming to those that intend to do us any harm."

"Pretty effective," Lee said and downed his drink. "I haven't tasted anything that pure even on my own planet. Take all my blood if you like!"

Despite how much the cart bounced around the road, Dane felt a certain sense of safety. The fires that had started to rage behind them seemed distant. The creatures in the cart came across as friendly, and Dane found that relaxing.

He closed his eyes and listened to the rumble of the road.

***

The cart rolled away and they followed the creatures to a wide expanse of lush grass. People moved freely among other creatures. Huts with smokestacks were scattered throughout the field. Everyone that passed Dane's eyes, that was human, looked deformed to him. An extra arm here or their heads may have been misshapen. However, after a few moments of walking through the small town, Dane realized that he was the outsider here. Yet, despite this, every man, woman, and arachnid-like creature they passed either waved or smiled to them—a few even stopped to introduce themselves.

The creature's led them to a small cluster of people and other arachnids. A stage built from wood stood in the middle of the field. On it were three dancers moving to and from one end of the stage to the other by hopping and twirling, until finally, they came together at the end to form a masterful totem pole of bodies.

Off to the side, Dane saw people openly making love. Unlike the Room of Aphrodite, their eyes were clear. They fed into the energy of one another with urgency, but also with focus. There was intent and passion in their eyes, something that Dane had never seen in the glazed over pits of his former crewmates. Music rang out from the stage and a man with stretched out cranium began playing an instrument that elicited the sound of wind chimes.

"It's beautiful, right?"

"Yes," Dane said.

"Remember there are other places just like this," Scarlet said. "Ones that will cease to exist if we let King Space Void continue."

"What can we do about these people?"

"We kill the Master everyone benefits from it."

Scarlet turned and walked away, leaving Dane to contemplate the fact that their mission wasn't over, although his body ached for it to be.

A hand grazed his shoulder.

Dane turned to see a woman standing behind him. Her ears were long, tapered, and speared with metal rods. It took him a moment to realize it was one of the dancers from the stage.

"I don't think I've seen you before." She held her hand out.

"I'm not from here," Dane said, taking her hand.

"Zaria, Welcome."

Dane's face flushed. His tongue felt like a lead slug.

"Do you like music?"

"I do. Whatever that is," Dane pointed at the triple-stacked machine with black and white keys on stage, "sounds beautiful."

"Would you like to sit and listen?"

"I'd love that."

She led him to the front of the stage where the music caressed his ears. He closed his eyes and thought of drifting in a pool of water. Together they sat and listened for hours.

When it ended, he followed her through a cluster of trees, hypnotized by the way she carried herself. Her laugh brought a smile to his face.

She stopped at a small clearing where he let himself be drawn down on top of her. She kissed his sealed, but still healing wounds, never broke eye contact with her. And when he entered the space between her thighs, Dane's world exploded.

Dane thought he had known passion in the safe, sanitary walls of the Aphrodite, but as Zaria brought her lips to his; as their hips moved in sync with one another, Dane knew that for the first time in his life he was experiencing something genuine; something real.

***

Screaming filled the air. Dane sat up. Dozens of the exploding spiders now filled the air. Except this time they didn't expel the same yellow liquid that the others had. Instead the horizon was a somber blue. Several of the arachnids dropped from the trees and scurried off toward the sound. Had they been watching them, Dane wondered.

When they parted through the trees, Scarlet and Lee were waiting for him. A wagon was parked next to them. Dane didn't need Scarlet to explain to him that it was time to leave. More of the eight-legged creatures launched themselves into the air. The tops of the human scarecrows were ablaze.

One of the arachnids stopped in front of them. "There's a man burning down our sanctuary. Do you know who this is?"

"No. Last I checked no one was following us."

Dane knew that was a lie. From the moment the Machine world began falling apart, he knew something was after them.

67

That the Master would not let them get to their destination without putting roadblocks in their way.

"Our land was fine until you showed up. Now look at it. You've brought death with you."

To add emphasis to its point, the spider lifted a muck-covered limb up. Dane looked down to his feet to see what looked like liquefied tar leaking through the soil, pooling around his boots.

The ground gurgled and belched. Viscous black fluid sprayed into the air. Zaria fell backward into a growing puddle. She hit the ground with a splash, cried out. Dane moved to try and pull her out of the sludge, but two heavy arms wrapped around his waist.

"Get in the wagon." Lee's breath was hot against Dane's ear. "You can't help her."

Dane stomped forward a few feet, but the perverted green man's grip was too strong. Dane couldn't take his eyes off the woman he'd been making love to just an hour before. Her eyes bulged with fear. She reached a weak hand out to Dane. Bubbles of oil popped in her mouth as she tried to call out for help, but only managed to elicit a weak cry, like a dying cat.

"You don't need to see this," Lee said and began to turn him away.

"Let him watch," Scarlet said.

Zaria's arm began to rise as she sunk deeper. Dane saw the glint in her eyes, a microsecond of a twinkle, before her head submerged.

"Do you see this, Dane?"

Scarlet kept talking even though Dane didn't answer. Tears dripped down his cheeks.

"This is what will happen to the planet that I showed you. If King Space Void doesn't devour it, he will find a way to enslave it or later ruin it, just as he has done here. Remember this, too, when we finally come face-to-face with *him*."

Scarlet's voice was angry.

The pale arm sunk to the elbow, the forearm, and then disappeared.

Dane felt nothing.

***

When they were far enough away from the malignant black pools, the wagon stopped in front a large spherical tube. Dane recognized it immediately as one of the elevators from the gut. Had the Master been coming down here? Why hadn't there been an elevator in the junkyard? More importantly, why'd they take those fucking stairs if there were just an elevator running through it? The questions piled on the further they went.

"This has been here since we can remember," said the Arachnid. "We don't know what it is or how it works. Every so often it will cause earthquakes, but other than that it seems to serve no primary purpose."

"I know what it is," Dane said and moved around it. "It's one of our elevator shafts." His hands moved over the smooth, rounded surface. It was definitely part of King Space Void, but there was no discernible way to pop it open. It lacked the markings Dane was used to seeing; dials for moving from floor to floor.

"Should we just blow the damn thing open," Lee asked.

"I don't think that'll be necessary," said a voice behind them.

They all turned to see Grier standing behind them. He appeared to have taken a spill in the black liquid, but that didn't keep Dane from seeing the crusted lines of blood from dozens of bite marks on his face. A good chunk of his lower lip had been gnawed to a ragged tuft of flesh.

His fist, wrapped in blood-soaked gauze, held three leashes. Three of Dane's old co-workers were collared and eager to reach them. They snarled and drooled, hungry. Behind Grier were two of the Machine Gods workers that looked slapped together at the last minute. Their heads were rusted bolts and their core systems pulsed with energy.

"We're taking that elevator back to the gut and you're going in the fucking 'grynder!"

Grier pulled what looked like a small detonator from inside one of his junkyard bodyguards.

The shaft lit up and shook the ground. Seeing this as an opportunity to strike the arachnid leapt onto the engine-block of the closest bodyguard. Seconds later it burst like a boil. Alien blood leaking into its internal workings, the body guard swung its large arms.

Grier dove out of the strike-zone, but one of his dogs caught a face full of welded metal. Nose, eyes, and teeth came screaming out the back of the man's head.

Behind them the elevator doors slid open.

The second guard responded to the threat, drove a fist studded with screwdrivers into its brethren's chest. Screeching metal rang out as the makeshift daggers were wrenched free from the bulky metallic box.

Two hands pulled Dane to his knees. Teeth nipped at his ear, while a hand grabbed at his crotch. The woman on his back growled and grunted in his ear, as she tried to devour him and get him off at the same time.

Dane snapped his head back. Cartilage crunched from the impact and the weight fell off. The other sex-crazed animal came at him on all fours, but suddenly buckled and yelped. Scarlet drove a large trunk of wood into its side.

Before racing into the elevator, Dane turned to yell for Lee, who was doing a pretty good job of dodging the machine guard's attacks. His coat tails flung behind him with every move, like a hero's cape.

"Let's go," Dane shouted.

Lee pivoted away from the guard and ran toward them. Dane's hear beat faster in his ribcage, as the flat-faced and one-eyed friend of theirs pitched forward.

Lee hit the ground face-first. Grier pushed himself up from the ground, grabbed the collar of Lee's coat and brought him to his feet. The machine guard stomped forward, rammed a fist into Lee's back. The sound that came from his lips would haunt Dane for the rest of his life.

Dane continued to watch. Another arachnid hitched itself to the last machine guard, exploded in a hail of green acidic slime. Dane wanted to reach out and grab Lee's hand, pull him into the elevator with him, but it was too late, Scarlet was dragging him back, and then the doors were closing, erasing the scene before them.

Chapter Twelve

The elevator opened to a long hallway. Thick pulsing veins lined the corroded, leaky walls.

Pools of slime stuck to the bottom of Dane's shoes. The floor, walls, and ceiling were studded with pulsating tumors that ranged in size from fists to large boulders. Across their surface were puffy slits that wept thick, milky teardrops, while others sat, motionless and benign.

Dane had always assumed that the above levels would be nicer, more pristine and fitting for the Master. From where he stood he saw nothing but a landscape of disease. One thing did catch his attention, however. Off to the side one of the lumps began to emit puffs of steam that smelled faintly like what they smoked from the hookahs in the Aphrodite.

The tumor belched. Its wet lips vibrated and sent a cloud of swampy mist toward them. Scarlet dug into her bag, pushed a mask into his hand.

"Put it on."

Dane didn't argue. He pulled the heavy rubber mask over his mouth and nose. It sat awkwardly like a blue half-mask, but it kept the pheromone smog from creeping into their nostrils and mouth. Neither spoke as they wound their way through the cancerous floor to a tube in the middle of the room.

"You're not supposed to be here," said a voice from behind them.

Dane knew that the scout ships were required to bring back different kind of specimens, mostly health aids for

King Space Void. He imagined scientists boxing up samples of soil or scraping bacteria from oceanic depths. He didn't expect to see anything like the two creatures standing behind them. Golden orbs looked out at them from bony sockets. A bridge of skin tethered them to one another. Set inside the veiny bond was a toothless mouth.

"You're not one of the doctors. What are you doing here?"

"We want to see the Master," Scarlet said.

"I'm afraid that's impossible."

"Why?"

"You only see the Master when he wants to be seen."

Scarlet, tired and weary, raised her gun.

The look on her face must have been enough, because four arms went up at once. "On second thought, I am not a gatekeeper, so, please, go as you wish."

"You're not going to try and stop us," Scarlet asked.

The lips formed a tight line. "The Master is not aware of the state that we are in. We can continue to produce as much of the aphrodisiacs as possible, but we are slowing down... dying. And without my partner, Lee, well there's not much we can do."

"What are all of these?" Dane gestured at the labial tumors.

The mouth laughed. "This is where your aphrodisiacs come from. The cakes and tobaccos that you are so fond of on your days off are the excrement of these pods. We modify them of course. They're mixed with milk from Lee's trunks. Undiluted consumption would likely kill you."

Bile rose up in Dane's throat. How much of these things had he ingested over the years? He thought he could feel bacteria growing in his throat, creating colonies of tumors.

"You knew Lee," Dane asked and hung his head.

Two sets of shoulders slumped. The mouth became a tight line.

"Well, I guess that was inevitable. Lee always wanted to do and see more. Anyway, as I was saying. The Master had no idea what he was doing when he agreed to allow the vaginal sacs to bond with his flesh. The other bodies he tested on were successful. "For example, Gardenia has been with us a very long time." One of the silent twins attached to the mouth waved to the darkness. "It's safe, sweetheart, join us."

There was a shuffling sound and then a wet smack and tear, like roots being uprooted from mud. A form took shape in the darkness. Dane looked on with awe as Gardenia moved closer to them. It had been human, or at least vaguely humanoid at some point, but now without the aid of legs it had to drag itself toward them on purplish fists. Tangles veins dragged behind it.

"Gardenia, these two want to talk to the Master. I'm going to go with them. That leaves you in charge. Are you okay with that?"

Dane didn't know if the creature had any eyes or a mouth, but it emitted a low whine and nodded its mottled head up and down.

"Good," the mouth said.

"We don't even know your name," said Scarlet.

"Oh, forgive me. I seem to have lost my manners. My name is Keele, and I would be happy to join your small group in order to get some answers."

Chapter Thirteen

Everything you have been doing has been at the expense of someone else's misery. Your life's daily routine, your work, and the days you have spent on King Space Void are nothing more than small building blocks of destruction. You're a cog, Dane Shipps; Worker 1255. And you've been lied to.

You are no one.

Scarlet jabbed Dane in the side, breaking his thoughts. "Hey, you with us?"

Dane pulled the rubber mask down. "What? Yeah, sorry. I get a little loopy sometimes."

As they closed in on the Master—a difficult feat for two individuals welded together by biology—they came to learn a lot about what Dane's false idol had been doing. According to their new companion, the Master was very aware of the different dimensions within itself.

When Scarlet questioned Keele about his choice to desert his people, it was met with a dual shoulder shrug. "It beat death."

"You never felt bad that you agreed to do this," Scarlet asked.

"Never gave it a second thought. Survival makes one do things they didn't know they were capable of. If you were presented with the same choices, what would you do?"

"I'd die."

Dane didn't doubt for a second that Scarlet was telling the truth. Her and her group had infiltrated King Space Void fully expecting to die within its flesh-coated walls. It took a lot of guts to decide that your life was worth trading, so that billions could survive.

In reality, Dane was the only one here that was a true traitor. He'd turned his back on his vows as a citizen of King Space Void. By doing so, those aboard, the workers, the folks from other worlds, were all doomed. The word hypocrite flashed in his mind. Every action brought three more conflicting questions to his mind. Yet, in his heart, Dane felt that his journey was justified. If his fellow brothers and sisters aboard King Space Void had seen the pillaged landscapes and abducted creatures exploited for no other reason than to keep the populace subdued, they too, would reach the same conclusions he had.

Dane pitied some of them even. They'd never have someone to lift the veil from their eyes to show them that there was more to the world they knew.

"Where are we," Dane asked.

Pink and yellow plants grew from between limp waves of grass. Small circular pools were scattered around them. Dane thought he could see shadows underneath the surface of the bubbling liquids. Vines above swayed and dripped clear fluid. One closest to him bulged as something made its way down the pipeline. Then with a wet cough, the tube spit out a ball of jelly, an embryo wedged in its center.

"Anyone going to pick that up," Dane asked.

" The Tesstrianas collect them when the Master is ready to farm them out," Keele said. He then turned and shouted, "Where is the triage?!"

The pools began to spill over and three women emerged from their depths. Long blonde hair rolled over pendulous breasts. Their lower halves covered by black underwear.

"You all have the same name?"

"We share a collective conscious," the one in the middle

said. "It's easier to have three bodies rather than one."

"They help care for the new citizens of King Space Void after they're born," Keele explained. "When they're old enough they're sent to education where they learn the purpose of their lives."

Dane scoffed. Their only purpose aboard the ship was to work and then die. Only, the Master's teachers sold it as spiritual enlightenment, that their worth in the afterlife was based on their ability to feed the machine.

"So, you're the incubators," Scarlet said to the triage.

They shook their heads in unison. "No quite the opposite. Follow us. You're here so we might as well show you."

The Tresstrianas turned and moved toward a wall of plants that parted easily. Dane, Scarlet, and Keele followed. Behind the foliage sat a purple pod that resembled an upright squash with the top split open. Birthing tendrils snaked out of it and disappeared above. Standing around the pod were three naked men. They approached the pod, pushed their cocks into the soft accepting body before them.

The men braced themselves, bucked their hips into it, until finally they fell back, sweat-covered and spent. Their eyes crystallized honey.

"So they volunteer for this?"

"No," said the closest. Tesstriana. "Donors are selected at random and then disposed of."

"How," Dane asked.

"Watch."

Sections of the pod began to peel away like a banana to reveal a thick translucent stalk. Inside of it were blue and red veins wrapping around dozens of tiny embryos floating in amniotic fluid. Suddenly, the flaps belched and a gluey red substance drew up from the middle of the leaves like taffy. Dane found himself transfixed as the sentient matter reached out to the naked men before it, attached itself to their faces and mid-sections, and drew them into the slime-slick jaws splayed out like a beautiful, but torturous bed.

The men were enveloped. Gracefully the creature folded itself back up to digest the mulch it had created and feed the growing babies inside of it.

"What's the point of this if they're all going to die?"

The Tresstriana's smirked. "You know this answer to this. They can work. They can find new ways to keep King Space Void alive until we reach the Edge, or they can donate themselves to the 'grynder. Because, when all is said and done, we feed the machine."

"They should have a choice in what they're doing," Dane said.

"Choice is a luxury. One most of us do not have. They should count themselves lucky they're allowed to live at all. Like all creatures, they're doomed from the womb."

The Tresstriana's waited for Dane's response, eager to hear a rebuttal. He didn't take the bait. It was a bitter sentiment from someone that knew they're life was destined for an unhappy ending. However she didn't seem determined to stop them from their journey.

Scarlet looked around. "I don't see a way out of here."

Tesstriana pointed to an area covered by an entanglement of vines.

"It's further back. The Master wanted to keep it hidden in case anyone from the gut came poking around. May I ask you, why do you want to see him?"

"They think they're going to save the fucking world."

Grier emerged pushed himself through the hanging plants to sour another presumably peaceful. Straddled to his back was one of workers he had collared and leashed earlier. Her tongue left a trail of saliva as it dug into his ear.

A good portion of Grier's clothes were shredded. His body was covered in bite and claw marks that dribbled blood, but the worst thing about Grier showing up was what he carried in his hand.

Grier clutched a handful of Lee's hair. Tendons and skin dangled from the neck stump. He grinned when he saw the disgust on Dane's face. Yeah, you think you're going to get far, Shipps?"

Grier tossed Lee's head at their feet.

"Oh, fuck this guy," Scarlet moaned and pulled the gun from her waistband.

Grier ducked, but his human backpack picked the wrong time to look up her lover's neck. The blast sent her face rocketing up to the ceiling like a wet trash bag in the wind.

Grier shouldered the body off and stepped forward. Scarlet fired again. He ducked and the grass covered wall beyond went up in flames. Dane figured she must have hit one of the birth canals because gobs of unborn specimens spilled down in fat tear drops.

Taking her time, Scarlet lined up the shot, but just as she was about to pull the trigger, the Tresstrianas screamed all at once. One of them reached over and grabbed Scarlet's wrist. The shot went wild, hit Keele in the mouth, and the mouth went up in a red mist.

"This is not a place for violence," the Tesstriana's screamed.

Scarlet lost her patience, hit the closest Tresstriana in the mouth. The other two took a step back, fearful.

Dane was still trying to process Keele's death when Grier came at him. Wind rushed out of his mouth as his former crewmate tackled him to the ground. Dane heard the cartilage in his nose snap and pop as Grier laid into him. Teeth vacated his gum line. His vision turned into a grease-streaked window.

After a moment the pain began to subside. Dane felt himself falling away, which was odd, he thought to himself because there was solid ground underneath him. He went with it, though, happy the lights in his head were starting to flicker on and off with every hit.

Suddenly the weight was off him. Grier's face faded away. He closed his eyes to try and bring himself back around, but the hammering didn't subside. Nonetheless he was no longer being pummeled.

The fight unfolded in front of him. Scarlet straddled Grier by the chest, much like she did when showing him her world. Hope flickered in Dane's chest. Maybe she would convert Grier, too. They needed someone like him on their side, arrogant and excited by violence.

However, Dane didn't remember his body shuddering the way Grier's did when Scarlet put her lips to his. His face began to bubble, pop, and leak like ruptured pustules. When she finished, Scarlet strode to where Dane was laying.

"Get up."

Scarlet's face came into view. Her eyes were blazing and looked like they were housing small fire pits. It made him want to push himself into gear. With Scarlet's help, Dane got to his feet and together they made for the wall of foliage.

Chapter Fourteen

The hallway was a maze. They turned right, left, and then climbed up a steep rise where finally the floor flattened out into a giant space that resembled the gut in that a set of circular walkways were set above them. What actually intrigued Dane, though, was the fact that he was staring up at a large pulsating muscle. Blues and purples pumped through various tubes that flowed from the walls and into what could only be the heart of King Space Void. Several multi-armed workers performed maintenance across the surface to ensure maximum performance.

They stood in silence and watched the workers skitter across the massive organ. Dane's work down in the gut had been hard, but nothing like what he was seeing. This was intricate, detailed work; not shoveling debris or pulling a series of levers for twelve hours at a time. There was artistry to what they were witnessing. Each worker was valuable to the functionality of the great pump before them. Dane figured these were more of the Master's valued workers— the ones that were harder to replace.

"I've never seen one of these before," Dane said.

"What do you mean?"

"A heart." Dane put his hand over his chest.

Scarlet nodded. "The other capsule. Was there someone in the pod when they found it?"

Dane thought of the melting man. How he had somehow come undone within seconds was something Dane would never forget. Scarlet didn't need to live with that kind of memory, knowing that someone she knew had ended their lives in such a gruesome way.

"It was empty."

"You're lying to me."

Dane flinched at the accusation, but didn't bother refuting her statement. It'd just make him sound worse. No point in upsetting the one person that had saved his life twice now. The realization brought another point to the forefront of Dane's mind. Every situation they had been in since Dane helped Scarlet out of the ducts, she had gotten them out of. Not once did Dane ever do more than throw a weak punch or hightail it in the opposite direction, his manhood shrinking in the process.

"What happened?"

"You don't want to know."

Again, Scarlet turned to look at him, as if to say one more dumb statement and your ass is getting left behind.

"I've never seen anything like it. The Master deals with punishment quietly. But this time, I think he wanted to make a statement. So they lowered the man down into the gut inside this cage, so that he could—"

"Feed the machine," Scarlet interrupted.

"Yes," Dane said, solemn.

"Is that what happened to, Yakob? He became a sacrifice?"

Dane didn't want to know the man's name. It brought him closer to the dead. His mind actively tried to shove that tidbit of information out, but failed. Dane wondered what kind of a life Yakob had before entering the jaws of King Space Void. Had he and Scarlet been lovers? Perhaps they were from the same sect of their society and the two had simply developed an ongoing relationship.

"Not exactly. He…how do I say this? He melted."

Scarlet narrowed her eyes. "And you saw this happen?"

"Yes. He was yelling and screaming, but then suddenly he just stopped, and split apart. Whatever was in his system briefly shut King Space Void down."

"The power outage."

"Exactly. Any idea how something like that can happen."

Scarlet looked back at the heart, unscrewed the cap from a small bottle, and emptied its contents into the swirling brown bile below them.

"I have a few ideas about how that could happen. We should keep going, though. Do you see a way out of here?"

Dane looked around, found zilch for an exit. "Nothing."

Scarlet threw a leg over the side of the railing and shimmied to the left, keeping her eyes in front of her. For someone that had been near death hours ago, she moved fast and with little effort.

He followed Scarlet along the railing until they found a thick pipe jutting out of the wall and into the side of King Space Void's heart. They leapt from the walkway. Scarlet executed a perfect landing, while Dane found that he didn't really care for the way his knee kissed his lower jaw. Teeth clacked and the faint hint of copper stroked at his tongue.

Dane followed Scarlet to where the pipe disappeared into the heart. He boosted her up first, enjoying the way the thick leather of her boots felt in his hand. Once at the top of the heart she reached down and pulled him up. The act made Dane feel slightly childish, but at the same time, he enjoyed the grip she had on his wrists. A part of him wished that he could experience something more intimate with her, feel her body, and perhaps share a moment of physical connection, like he had done with Zaria.

Maybe once they made it back to her planet, he told himself. They could lay out with one another in a field. Dane had always wanted to do something like lay out on the surface of a planet, looking up at the sky, planets, and stars rather than look at the pictures and art pieces that adorned different hallways and most of the wall space in the Aphrodite.

Dozens more tubes sprouted from the top of the heart and upwards. Few workers stopped to look at them standing there, lost. Close up, Dane could see that all of the workers looked exactly the same. Three arms on each side of their bodies. Bald with large obsidian eyes that bulged each time their sloped foreheads furrowed. Thick wads of spit hung down from their chins as they worked away, tightening bolts, or changing out smaller tubes.

Dane continued to observe the chamber. It hadn't been built for folks without extra appendages. "Unless one of us sprouts a few extra arms we are not getting out of here any time soon," Dane said. "What do you think?"

When Scarlet didn't respond Dane turned to find one of the workers standing a few feet away from them. It was bigger than the others by about at least three feet when it stood on two legs. Its throat was collared by yellow fur and in each hand it held a different tool. Something honey-colored dripped from its back-end.

"Hello, there," it said.

Chapter Fifteen

"I was giving some thought to bashing both your brains in," the creature said, "But then I thought to myself, why do that when I'm more curious about who you are."

Scarlet and Dane took a few steps back. Their weapons were long gone and he didn't think this was a fist fight either of them could win, even as a twosome.

"You, in the grey. You are one of the gut workers. I don't recognize your friend here, though. Too many bells and whistles on that outfit. Who are you?"

"I'm from one of the planets your ship intended to exterminate."

The creature belched. A curtain of thick yellow syrup spilled from its mouth as it laughed. "That is cute. I used to be like you, girl, but soon came to realize that this was a way better deal."

"This whole place is full of fucking cowards," Scarlet said.

Dane tried not to take the comment personally.

"Hardly. We were dying anyway. I took the path to life. Once we arrive at the Edge, though, we will have peace and the ability to roam free. Until then, we work for the dream until it becomes our reality."

The creature's hands clenched and unclenched the weapons it held. It was feeling them out. Trying to decide when would be the best time to strike and drag their bodies back down to the gut. Dane slowly moved between the worker and Scarlet; a weak gesture of masculinity and a poor attempt at trying to do something, but it was the best he could do.

From below came the sound of something splashing in the water. This averted the creature's attention for a moment. Dane lunged, palms out, and shoved as hard as he could. The creature fell backward, throwing three of the tools it held. Only the hammer connected and sent a shock of pain through Dane's shoulder.

The rest of the workers turned berserk in light of the assault on their foreman. They fell from the ceiling like refugees from an upset hornet's nest. Dane moved as fast as he could. Throwing wild punches that often didn't connect or hit home hard enough, but it at least stunned them enough so they didn't anticipate Dane's follow up tactic: shoving them off the heart.

One of the workers latched onto his back, bear-hugged him from behind. Pressure built in Dane's mid-section. He brought a boot down on the creature's foot, and a roar filled his ears, but he managed to loose himself from the grip and scramble forward. Underneath them the waters were rising. Whatever Scarlet had dropped into it was affecting King Space Void's fluids.

A few feet away, Scarlet was scooting backward, throwing glances over her shoulder. She stopped an inch from the edge. The foreman stomped forward. "It's not often I get to pull the legs off one of you types, sweetheart."

Dane watched, disgusted, as the stinger protruding from the foreman's back dribbled an excessive amount of fluid, leaving a slimy trail behind it. He knew that if he didn't get off his ass and act now, there'd be no Scarlet left for him to enjoy the stars with; no one to talk to about how beautiful the planets were from where they sat.

Dane sprinted toward the foreman. Ducked low and

caught it at the waist. Pain bloomed in his lower abdomen as the stinger dug into his flesh. The pain sent a shock through his system. The creature wrenched around, shoved Dane back. And before Dane could make another run at his opponent, the creature clipped him in the temple with one of the hammers it held.

Dane fell back, grabbed the foreman's wrist with his left hand as hard as he could. Wrist bones cracked like broken toothpicks. The foreman screamed in Dane's face, yellow spittle spraying his chin. From behind the foreman, Scarlet reached up, grabbed another arm, and yanked a long screwdriver from its grey hands.

Without missing a beat, she jammed the tool into his fur-lined throat. "You're going to take us to the Master."

Chapter Sixteen

They rode the foreman up a curved tube that led up into the wall. Scarlet never took the weapon away. Not when the creature's spine inverted from their weight, and not even when she forced him to knock on the Master's chambers. The double-door's parted and presented the Master's world to them.

Encased in a massive glass case was a ball of red and orange energy. Control panels wrapped around the interior. Two large windows looked out the expanse of the universe as King Space Void trudged on toward its next victim.

Standing next to the encased energy of the Master was a man dressed in a long white coat. A ribbed coil of metal ran from the back of his bald, liver-spotted head to a port at the bottom of the case. His eyes were downcast, ignoring the interlopers, while he made notes on a clipboard.

"Master…" The foreman said.

"You can leave, Sthura. Thank you. I'll take care of it from here."

The foreman had addressed the man in the coat as Master, yet, Dane's mind had a hard time comprehending the tired old man standing in front of them.

When the doors shut, Scarlet and Dane advanced on the Master. He casually pulled a device from his pocket, thumbed a dial, and a burst of electricity hit Scarlet in the chest. The warrior woman fell to the floor.

"Stop," The Master said, aiming the Taser at Dane. "I want to show you something."

Despite his newfound individuality, Dane froze. The Master pulled a cord from a box affixed to the energy case. At its tip were two prongs.

"Follow me."

Dane followed the Master to one of King Space Void's giant eyes. Before him was a mass of swirling colors. Planets floated like jewels. Off in the distance greys and purples bloomed. Dane's chest went tight. He had experienced beauty in the visions Scarlet showed him, but here was real beauty before him.

"Do you see it?"

"See what?"

"The Edge," the Master said. "We're almost there, Dane. We're almost there. Are you really going to stop us when we're this close?"

Dane stared harder at the expanse of the universe. There were golden clouds of gas; balls of flame; twinkles of silver against the never ending backdrop, like bits of glass glued to a black curtain. Any one of these things could have been the Edge and Dane wouldn't have known the difference. He'd never been shown the Edge, and he guessed that the Master was counting on that fact to earn himself more time.

Another lie, Dane thought.

"I don't want any more blood on my hands. This is wrong."

"Morality is a relative concept, Dane. Let me show you something else."

Dane didn't see the Master's right arm spring up until the prongs were already jammed into the back of his neck and his world turned to fire.

Chapter Seventeen

Who are you? asked the Master.

    Dane Shipps. Previously Worker 1255.

    No. Who are you?

    I am a man. I was born to Louise and Triana Shipps, Worker's 976 and 918.

    Are you sure about that?

    It's the memory I have. So it must be real.

    Hehe. Do you remember your parents?

    No. They died when I was a baby.

    Do you really think that's true?

    Images flashed. Bursts of moments from the past: Dane saw himself on his first clean up; Saw slender hands push him deeper as he lost his virginity in the Aphrodite; then swishing blue robes; disoriented voices murmuring commands about getting the right amount of flesh, mechanics, and memory right; flesh melts with steel; then a face the color of chestnuts with dark brown eyes looks back at him, solemn.

    I know that I possess certain traits that are not biological because of the accident.

    And do you know who you have to thank for your unique body?

    You

    Correct. You are more like me than you want to believe. Do you know who the woman is?

    I've never seen her before.

    Yes, you have. She was the woman who gave you life.

    That is not my mother. My mother was Lo—"

Another flood of images forced its way into Dane's head. The woman steps up to a birthing pod. It envelops her; strips away skin. Before his eyes, Dane watches this beautiful woman turned into a breeding machine.

Stop

Do you understand?

You're lying to me.

No. You're lying to yourself.

Dane's guts felt like lava. Heat flooded his face. The Master was starting to make him angry. The Master showed him another image. This time it was not of Dane, but of the Master walking through a dying world. Those around him beg as their skin sloughs off or their eyes pool in sockets to drip down tired faces.

Then suddenly the vision shift locales. The Master stands in the depths of a large cavern. He speaks to a shape in the darkness. Its voice rumbles and slithers.

"Your world has been invaded by a foreign disease. Why would we want it," asked the darkness.

"Because you can bring life to it again. You can help us destroy those that brought the plague."

"Don't lie to us. You care nothing for your species. This isn't about them. This is about you." The darkness snickers. "What's to stop us from taking it from you anyway?" "You are only a man."

"You could, yes, but think of all the things that I could do in your service. Grant me this request and I will live forever in your servitude."

The vision cut to black and then Dane was hovering above thousands like a spectral observer, while they built King Space Void. Another flash and the Master stood in front of a large, empty glass case.

"I'm ready," the Master said to the air.

Bursts of light fill the room. The Master is lifted off the floor by an unseen force. Tremors ripple through him, a thousand tiny earthquakes underneath the skin. Blood and flesh drip from the legs of pleated pants as an unseen god rips away the Master's life force. The empty vessel dropped and the glass case filled with an orange light.

"What will be done with my body?"

"It will be recycled. You will be able to create a better, newer bodies from here," said the darkness.

"And my people?"

The darkness laughed. "Still trying to convince us that you care about them? The already infected will not be able to join you, but those that are healthy are already being placed in the lower-levels."

"How will so few people keep my body moving," The Master asked his masters. "

"I'm glad you asked."

Dane could almost hear the darkness smile.

The visions brought Dane back to his trip through the birthing tube; doctors stood over him, retooling and refitting him for working in the gut; an explosion; Dane's lifeless body moves down a grease-streaked conveyor belt; three of the Machine God's lackeys hover over his half-maimed form, work feverishly to knit skin and bond flesh to metal; another machine makes cuts on Dane's face, shuffles the flesh around to make him presentable again.

In the ether of his fever dream, Dane felt like throwing up. Something heavy sat on his chest. He tried to scream, but no sound came out. This wasn't right. He had a family that he had been raised by. He grew up on King Space Void and worked hard.

Do you understand now?

I'm not real?

Oh, no, you are real. Your heart and your brain are unique to you. You're just modified so to speak and the timeline of your life is, shall we say, pre-determined, as is everything else you have been doing. You've been a slave, Dane Shipps, yes, but you owe me more than you think...

The prongs were yanked from his neck. The visions cut out and Dane was back at the head of King Space Void. He turned to look at the Master. This was it. The final moment he had been waiting for and he didn't know what to do. Part of him wanted to lash out, to slam his fists into the Master, and demand answers for the horrors he'd witnessed on their journey, but again, the words were clogged in Dane's throat.

Dane had expected more from the Master. After everything he had seen, Dane thought the Master's environment would be the most garish of them all. That wasn't the case, however. If anything, the membrane-like walls, pulsing with tumors and sores was just depressing.

"Get away from him," Scarlet said.

"Or what, bitch?" The Master turned and crossed his arms.

Scarlet didn't answer. The two stared at one another.

"Why don't you tell him your plan? You didn't come here to bring peace. You came here to kill us. All of us."

"What's he talking about?"

The Master's avatar sighed, took his glasses off, and rubbed his plum-sacked eyes.

"You dumb monkey. Let me ask you something since you've come all this way. What do you think is going to happen to you after? Do you think the two of you are just going to fly away on a chariot, spreading joy across the galaxy?"

Dane looked to Scarlet. She hung her head down.

"Oh, she didn't tell you, did she?"

The man laughed, cleared his throat, and spat at his feet. "You fucking pawn."

"What's he talking about?"

"I'm sorry," Scarlet said. "This is the end of the road for all of us."

"What about the places that exist here. There are places we can help. They can come with us."

Scarlet shook her head. "Dane, it doesn't matter. When it comes down to it, we're saving the last remaining planets that can create life. This one? This rolling death machine is a cancer. It's infected everything already in it."

Dane ground his teeth. "That's bullshit. I saw a great thing back there with Zaria. They deserve a chance."

Even as the words left his mouth, Dane knew that there was no chance of hope for them either. Every place they had visited on their journey, they had brought death to. Dane felt duped again. Embarrassment sank in. In his efforts to save, he'd only killed more innocent people. Twice he'd fallen for the whim of someone else.

He thought back to lying on the grass with Zaria, and the feeling of happiness that had pumped through him. In that moment everything was okay, but now here in front of the Master and everyone else, the memory was nothing more than a glimpse of the life Dane wasn't meant for.

He was an engine of death. And like all engines he was due to die sometime.

He might as well make it count.

Dane grabbed the tube connecting the Master's conscience to the body, swung hard. The frail man held his arms out, but it didn't do him any good. His face shattered against a console. Dane kicked the Master's leg out and then slammed the man against the window looking out at the galaxy. Blood smeared the glass.

The Master's breathing grew heavy. "Stop. You don't know what you're doing. You'll kill us all."

"Yeah, well, there's nothing left in this fucking place worth saving anymore."

Dane put his knee in between the Master's shoulder blades, pulled as hard as he could on the tube embedded into his skull. It tore away from the flesh with ease.

The ball of energy went crazy. Lines of electricity batted at the inside of the cell, it grew in intensity as Dane smashed every machine surrounding it, severing all of the Master's connections to the rest of the ship.

When he was finished the room was full of smoke. Dane bent down to help Scarlet up and together they limped toward the windows. Scarlet slipped her hand into his. Fists beat against the double doors. This wasn't how Dane had wanted it to end. He'd hoped the rest of King Space Void wouldn't have to suffer, but Scarlet was right—this was the end of the journey.

King Space Void began its fast but endless descent. They fell through dead stars and supernovas. The inside of the head felt like a sauna. Beneath them the body of King Space Void began to fall apart. Dimensions and civilizations were crushed. Death had always been a faraway concept for Dane, but here he was, racing to it, welcoming it.

Dane realized there was no right way to do this. In saving dozens of planets, they assigned other worlds to death. They couldn't bring King Space Void anywhere, though. Its entire body was corrupted, unsalvageable. No matter where they went, the body of King Space Void was toxic. This was the only way to end it.

Chapter Eighteen

Dane Closed his eyes as King Space Void lost all power, plummeted into darkness.

And in his mind, they went to the Edge.

Epilogue

The planet is lush. Its surface a light pink. Yellow and purple roses grow from long-armed plants that bend back in the slight breeze, so that if anyone had been looking, they could see the full beauty of life before them. Specks of dust fall softly onto thin, dew-spotted petals and fertile ground where hundreds of years later, two more roses will bloom.

One red.

One blue.

Anthony Trevino is the product of too much *Tales from the Crypt* and not enough socializing during his formative years. He prefers dogs to just about any other creature, and loves rooting through the garbage to steal your most intimate secrets. He's currently trapped fighting for his life in a rundown arcade room with only two shotguns left. Please send more shotguns.

The New Bizarro Author Series

2009-2010
Carnageland by D.W. Barbee
Naked Metamorphosis by Eric Mays
Sex Dungeon for Sale by Patrick Wensink
Rotten Little Animals by Kevin Shamel

2010-2011
How to Eat Fried Furries by Nicole Cushing
Muscle Memory by Steve Lowe
Felix and the Sacred Thor by James Steele
Love in the Time of Dinosaurs by Kirsten Alene
Uncle Sam's Carnival of Copulating Inanimals
    by Kirk Jones
The Egg Said Nothing by Caris O'Malley
Bucket of Face by Eric Hendrixson

2011-2012
A Hollow Cube is a Lonely Space by S.D. Foster
Lepers and Mannequins by Eric Beeny
Party Wolves in My Skull by Michael Allen Rose
Seven Seagulls for a Single Nipple
    by Troy Chambers
Gigantic Death Worm by Vince Kramer
The Placenta of Love by Spike Marlowe
Trashland A Go-Go by Constance Ann Fitzgerald
The Crud Masters by Justin Grimbol

2012-2013
Gutmouth by Gabino Iglesias
Janitor of Planet Anilingus
    by Andrew Wayne Adams
House Hunter S.T. Cartledge
Avoiding Mortimer by J.W. Wargo
Her Fingers by Tamara Romero
Kitten by G. Arthur Brown

2013-2014
The Mondo Vixen Massacre by Jamie Grefe
The Cheat Code for God Mode by Andy De Fonseca
Babes in Gangland by Bix Skahill
8-bit Apocalypse by Amanda Billings
Grambo by Dustin Reade
There's No Happy Ending by Tiffany Scandal
The Church of TV as God by Daniel Vlasaty

2014-2015
SuperGhost by Scott Cole
Pax Titanus by Tom Lucas
Deep Blue by Brian Auspice

2015-2016
King Space Void by Anthony Trevino
Rainbows Suck by Madeleine Swann
Arachnophile by Betty Rocksteady
Benjamin by Pedro Proenca
Rock 'n' Roll Head Case by Lee Widener
Slasher Camp for Nerd Dorks by Christoph Paul
Elephant Vice by Chris Meekings
Pixiegate Madoka by Michael Sean Le Sueur
Towers by Karl Fischer

Praise for
Carlton Mellick III

"Easily the craziest, weirdest, strangest, funniest, most obscene writer in America."
—*GOTHIC MAGAZINE*

"Carlton Mellick III has the craziest book titles... and the kinkiest fans!"
—CHRISTOPHER MOORE, author of *The Stupidest Angel*

"If you haven't read Mellick you're not nearly perverse enough for the twenty first century."
—JACK KETCHUM, author of *The Girl Next Door*

"Carlton Mellick III is one of bizarro fiction's most talented practitioners, a virtuoso of the surreal, science fictional tale."
—CORY DOCTOROW, author of *Little Brother*

"Bizarre, twisted, and emotionally raw—Carlton Mellick's fiction is the literary equivalent of putting your brain in a blender."
—BRIAN KEENE, author of *The Rising*

"Carlton Mellick III exemplifies the intelligence and wit that lurks between its lurid covers. In a genre where crude titles are an art in themselves, Mellick is a true artist."
—*THE GUARDIAN*

"Just as Pop had Andy Warhol and Dada Tristan Tzara, the bizarro movement has its very own P. T. Barnum-type practitioner. He's the mutton-chopped author of such books as *Electric Jesus Corpse* and *The Menstruating Mall*, the illustrator, editor, and instructor of all things bizarro, and his name is Carlton Mellick III."
—*DETAILS MAGAZINE*

Also by Carlton Mellick III

Satan Burger
Electric Jesus Corpse
Sunset With a Beard (stories)
Razor Wire Pubic Hair
Teeth and Tongue Landscape
The Steel Breakfast Era
The Baby Jesus Butt Plug
Fishy-fleshed
The Menstruating Mall
Ocean of Lard (with Kevin L. Donihe)
Punk Land
Sex and Death in Television Town
Sea of the Patchwork Cats
The Haunted Vagina
Cancer-cute (Avant Punk Army Exclusive)
War Slut
Sausagey Santa
Ugly Heaven
Adolf in Wonderland
Ultra Fuckers
Cybernetrix
The Egg Man
Apeshit
The Faggiest Vampire
The Cannibals of Candyland
Warrior Wolf Women of the Wasteland
The Kobold Wizard's Dildo of Enlightenment +2
Zombies and Shit
Crab Town
The Morbidly Obese Ninja
Barbarian Beast Bitches of the Badlands
Fantastic Orgy (stories)
I Knocked Up Satan's Daughter
Armadillo Fists
The Handsome Squirm
Tumor Fruit